THE MULTIPLYING
MENACE

Coming soon:

The Shape-Shifter's Curse

THE MULTIPLYING
MENACE

A Magic Repair Shop Book

Amanda Marrone

Aladdin

New York London Toronto Sydney

ALADDIN

An imprint of Simon & Schuster Children's Publishing Division

1230 Avenue of the Americas, New York, NY 10020

First Aladdin paperback edition June 2010

Copyright © 2010 by Amanda Marrone

All rights reserved, including the right of reproduction in whole or in part in any form.

ALADDIN is a trademark of Simon & Schuster, Inc., and related logo is a registered trademark of Simon & Schuster, Inc.

For information about special discounts for bulk purchases, please contact Simon & Schuster Special Sales at 1-866-506-1949 or business@simonandschuster.com.

The Simon & Schuster Speakers Bureau can bring authors to your live event. For more information or to book an event contact the Simon & Schuster Speakers Bureau at 1-866-248-3049 or visit our website at www.simonspeakers.com.

Designed by Mike Rosamilia

The text of this book was set in Centaur MT.

Manufactured in the United States of America 0710 OFF

2 4 6 8 10 9 7 5 3 1

Library of Congress Control Number 2009934392

ISBN 978-1-4169-9033-8

ISBN 978-1-4391-5822-7 (eBook)

For Max and Merry,
who can be magical when they want to be.

Big, huge love for my agent, Wendy Schmalz, and my editor, Kate Angelella, for seeing the magic in the repair shop—even if they don't like cockroaches. Thanks to my husband, Joe, for helping out while I was holed up in my office working. Thanks to Nina Nelson, Naomi Panzer, and Pam Foarde for their help, support, and editing eyes. Thanks to everyone at Aladdin for making Maggie's adventures come to life, and a shout-out to Brandon Dorman for his fabulous cover—it's amazing seeing my favorite characters come to life!

THE MULTIPLYING
MENACE

1

Because of Cockroaches

I sat outside Mrs. Stearns's office, waiting to hear my fate. I was pretty sure this was the first time in history a kid had gotten in trouble for ruining the Fifth Grade End-of-the-Year Celebration. According to a number of my classmates, I had upended a container of cockroaches on top of Roxie JoŸson's head before running out into the hall and pulling the fire alarm.

I had pulled the alarm—but only to buy myself some time to think, and honestly, the part about me bringing in a box of roaches to get back at Roxie was a much safer explanation than what had *really* happened.

I stared at the closed door, listening to the angry, muffled conversation on the other side. My parents had been in there for more than an hour, and I'd made out the word "expulsion" no less than four times.

The secretary, Mrs. Beamer, sat at her desk typing, but she looked up every few minutes to shake her head and glare at me like *I* was a cockroach. I wanted to tell her the whole thing was a horrible accident. That the wish I'd made had just slipped out after Roxie had humiliated me in front of the *entire* fifth grade.

I wanted to tell Mrs. Beamer how extra careful I'd been over the years to not say the word *wish* in public— and how I never, ever would've said it if I'd known Roxie's hair would disappear along with the roaches.

I squeezed my eyes shut to erase the picture of Roxie's bald head from my mind. Mrs. Stearns had insisted I take a "long, hard look" at a sobbing Roxie so I could see "the devastation" I'd caused with my "little prank," while the school nurse, Mrs. Pope, had said she was sure it was an extreme allergic reaction to cockroaches that had made Roxie's hair spontaneously fall out.

I leaned over and put my head in my hands. How had I let this happen? How could I have slipped up in front of everyone? The only good thing was that nobody knew my secret—nobody knew my wishes really came true.

As I sat across from Mrs. Beamer, I remembered the disastrous wish I'd made six years ago. My parents are entomologists, or in other words, *big, fat bug nuts*, and we'd stopped for the night on the way home from the twenty-fifth annual Putnam County Cockroach Appreciation Conference in Texas. It was my birthday, and I wasn't exactly happy spending what should've been the most exciting day of the year besides Christmas surrounded by scientists applauding the virtues of the world's most indestructible insect.

To make it up to me, my parents surprised me in our hotel room with a little pink cake topped with five blue candles.

"Blow them out and make a wish, Maggie," Mom said.

I let out a big puff, then closed my eyes. "I *wish* I had a monkey like the one in *Barty Bananas Saves the Circus*," I whispered.

My eyes flew open in a flash as the piercing cry of a chimpanzee, followed by my parents' screams, echoed in the room.

Right in front of me—sitting in my cake—was a scowling Barty Bananas wearing a yellow-and-red-striped vest. At first I was upset that the cake was ruined. I mean, even a five-year-old knows better than to eat something a monkey's butt has been sitting in. But then I looked at my parents.

Their eyes were wide, their mouths hung open; they looked like they were on the verge of keeling over.

I didn't understand. Yes, Barty Bananas *had* flattened the cake; but my wish had come true, so why weren't they happy?

The chimp howled again, dipped his long fingers in the cake, and flung a chunk at my dad—covering his face in a splatter of pink frosting. My mom shook her head disbelievingly and stared at Barty, opening and closing her mouth like a fish on dry land.

Barty bared his yellow teeth and shrieked. Dad's eyes rolled back, and he hit the floor like a coconut dropping from a palm tree.

It didn't take a genius to figure out that the problem wasn't Barty Bananas shaking his pink-frosted behind and flinging cake around the room. The problem was that my parents hadn't expected my wish to come true.

With my dad passed out and my mom looking like she might join him any second, I wished Barty and the mess away, and sat on the bed looking innocently at my magically repaired cake—candles still smoking.

Once my dad came to, he started talking about group hallucinations and something called Legionnaires' disease that's common at conventions. My mom kept asking me how Barty had appeared, but I pretended I didn't know what they were talking about.

The cake went uneaten, and I learned an important lesson—people like magic in storybooks, far away from real life.

From that point on, I was always on my best behavior, because I was a little worried about what parents did with kids who could conjure up crazed monkeys. I even had nightmares about being sent to a home for the magically insane.

So after Barty's appearance I tried not to wish for anything unless I was in my room with the door locked. And I didn't wish for anything big like a monkey—just candy and an occasional soda. Because besides insects, my parents are obsessed with healthy foods, and there's just so much chocolate-flavored tofu a kid can eat without craving the real thing.

There was also the time I wished up some earthworms to scare my babysitter, Ashley, who was more interested in texting her boyfriend than playing with me. She ended up with a lapful of garter snakes instead of worms—a classic example of how sometimes my wishes go wrong—and after that I realized I had to be extra, extra careful and keep my magic under wraps! And I'd been doing a great job, if I do say so myself—until today.

Finally, Mrs. Stearns's door opened, and I jumped up.

Mom and Dad looked as pale as they had when Barty had made his appearance.

"Let's go," Dad said. I gulped as I stared at a vein I'd never noticed before bulging on his forehead.

Mom turned to Dad. "Maybe Connecticut," she muttered.

My heart just about stopped. Connecticut was where Gram lived. Gram, who I only saw once a year when she'd come out for Thanksgiving. Gram, who'd never been a cookie-baking, huggy kind of grandmother. Gram, who never smiles.

"Connecticut?" I asked as we left the building.

Mom sighed. "Nothing's been decided, but we are in the difficult position of finding a new school for you next year."

We got in the car and drove home in silence.

Two weeks later my worst fear came true.

"I thought Connecticut was out! I thought you said there was a good chance I could get into Buxton Prep?"

"We can't afford the tuition," Dad said.

"My grades are pretty good—maybe I could get a scholarship?"

Mom shook her head. "I've already spoken to the admission officer. Expulsion from the Academy district disqualifies you from scholarship awards."

"Did you tell them Roxie had been bullying me?"

"Roxie's teasing does not excuse what you did, young lady!" Mom snapped.

I hung my head and, for the hundredth time this week, considered telling them the truth. "You could homeschool me," I said instead.

"Well, that would be rather difficult, considering your mother and I will be in South America."

My eyes nearly popped out of my head. "What?"

My parents exchanged looks. Mom nodded at Dad and they turned to face me.

"You know Professor Nelson," Dad said, "the head of the Entomology Department?"

I nodded as my stomach fluttered nervously.

"Well," Mom continued, "she received some grant money to do an insect species count in the Amazon."

I nodded again and felt a lump welling up in my throat.

"Professor Nelson had asked us to be on the team a few weeks ago," Mom said. "It was an incredible honor and an amazing chance to discover new species and maybe even a new cockroach. We told her we couldn't possibly go, but now . . ."

I shook my head in disbelief—first my friend Sarah had e-mailed to tell me her parents had forbidden her to come over anymore, and now my parents were abandoning me too.

"You're choosing *cockroaches* over me?"

"It's not like that at all," Dad said. "This is a once-in-a-lifetime opportunity for your mother and me. Besides, it'll give you a chance to get to know your grandmother better."

"But I don't want to get to know Gram better!"

Mom reached out and put her hand on my arm. "It's only for a year."

I yanked my arm away and stood up. "A *year*? I have to live with Gram for a *whole year*?"

"You can reapply to the Academy district after that," Mom said, "and by then I'm sure everyone will have had time to forget about what happened."

I rolled my eyes. Like anyone would ever forget Roxie's cockroach makeover. I already knew I could never go back to Academy, but I'd thought that if I *did* go to Connecticut, Mom and Dad would be coming with me.

I looked at my parents staring at me, and a tear tumbled down my cheek. "But why can't I come with you? I won't be any trouble, I swear!"

Mom sighed. "Oh, Maggie, the Amazon isn't exactly kid-friendly. Believe me, we thought long and hard about this. We wouldn't send you to your grandmother's if we didn't think you'd be happy there."

"And you won't go until just before school starts, so we'll have lots of time to be together," Dad said, like that would make everything okay.

"I can't believe you're doing this to me." I was so mad, I considered wishing up an encore performance from Barty Bananas! "How could you leave me to count a bunch of cockroaches—who even cares how many there are, anyway?"

"I know it's hard for someone your age to understand," Dad said. "But it's a very important biodiversity study, honey."

"This is an opportunity for you, too," Mom added. "A whole new state to explore, new friends to discover. It'll be a fresh start."

I brushed my blond bangs out of my eyes and folded my arms across my chest. "Oh, great—a fresh start with someone I see once a year."

Dad stood up and walked over to me. He wrapped his arms around me and I started cry. "I know you don't get to see your grandmother that often, but I think she's really looking forward to your stay."

Yeah, I was sure the woman who couldn't even be bothered to sign my birthday card was *really* looking forward to having me move in.

2

Gray Skies Are Gonna Clear Up

On August 27, my parents and I took off on separate planes from Denver International Airport. They warned me that while they'd try their best, communicating from the jungle might not always be possible. I'd just shrugged. They'd already made it clear what was important to them, and it wasn't me.

After my plane landed in Connecticut, I walked into the terminal feeling queasy from the turbulence, and hoped Gram would take one look at my greenish complexion and the lovey-dovey grandmother gene would finally kick into action.

I saw her standing off to the side of the gate. She was wringing her hands and her white hair was pulled back into a severe bun. There were no flowers, no balloons, no WELCOME, MAGGIE! sign anywhere in sight. But when she caught my eye, she waved. For a split second a smile broke out on her face and I got my hopes up.

Gram walked toward me and said, "Your plane was late. Is that your only bag?"

"Yeah," I said, readjusting my luggage strap over my shoulder. "Mom already sent most of my stuff in the mail."

"Well, good. That means we can skip the baggage claim, and if we're lucky, we'll beat the commuter traffic home."

That was it. No hug—not even a lipsticky kiss on the cheek. She started walking and I hustled to keep up, wondering if Gram didn't like kids in general or if there was just something about me that rubbed her the wrong way.

I couldn't believe I'd let Dad convince me that Gram was really looking forward to having me stay with her!

I bit my lip, trying to stop the tears pooling in my eyes.

As I followed Gram through the airport, I decided I *would* make a "fresh start"—only not the way Mom had in mind. It was time to take my magic off the back burner and have some fun. It wasn't like I needed to worry about Mom and Dad sending me away anymore; they'd already done it!

I considered wishing all of Mom and Dad's under-wear out of their suitcases—I even laughed to myself imagining bras, boxer shorts, and bikini briefs falling from their airplane somewhere over Brazil—but then I thought of something even better.

As I put my bag in the trunk of the taxi, I closed my eyes. *I wish something truly magical would happen.*

As the taxi pulled up to Gram's apartment build-ing, she closed her book and sighed. "Well, here we are."

I stepped out onto the sidewalk and shook my head. I knew city living would take some getting used to, but I felt claustrophobic with all of the buildings wedged right in next to one another. And after all the trees we'd passed on our way here—so different from the bare plains in Colorado—this treeless block was a major disappointment.

There was a boarded-up barber shop next to a small corner grocery store, and every telephone pole was plas-tered with flyers and announcements. One bright purple poster stood out over all of the rest: MILO THE MAGNIFI-CENT'S MAGICAL SUMMER SPECTACULAR.

I groaned. I'd been to plenty of so-called "magic" shows, and it'd be just my luck that some loser performing in downtown Bridgeport was how my *big* wish was going to come true.

"There's your room—first floor with the flowers in front of it," Gram said, pointing a gnarled hand.

I looked up at the faded, pink plastic poinsettias stuck into a sagging flower box.

Suddenly the window above my new room slid open, and a boy and a girl with purple-stained faces and hands popped out. "Mrs. Malloy!" the boy yelled, waving a grape ice pop at us. "Is that the Magnolia girl you were talking about?"

I turned to Gram and saw her lips turn into a smile. "Anthony, this is *Maggie*."

"Well, what the heck happened to Magnolia—did she get sick?" he asked. "I threw up three times yesterday; did she eat too many hot dogs too?"

"Maggie's her nickname, silly," the girl said. She took a dainty lick of her pop, then smiled at me. "I'm Anna Marie, and it is very pleasant to meet you." She stuck her tongue out at her brother. "I'm tellin' Momma you didn't do polite introductions!"

Anthony scowled at his sister, then stuck his thumb in his mouth.

"I was hoping you'd be littler," Anna Marie said to me. "I'm five!"

Anthony took his thumb out of his mouth and held out five purple fingers. "I'm five too." He took another lick of his pop and then inserted his thumb into his mouth again.

"Maggie, meet the Lubchek twins," Gram said.

Anna Marie twisted her head up and yelled, "Raphael! Magnolia's here!"

An older boy, with dark brown curls hanging in his eyes, pushed up the screen and leaned out the window on the third floor. "I told you a hundred times, Mrs. Malloy said her name was *Maggie!*" He smiled and waved to me. "I'm Raphael."

"Raphael Santos!" a voice called out behind him. "How many times do I have to tell you to stop hollering out the window? Get back in here and finish your work!"

Raphael rolled his eyes and brushed the curls off his forehead. "I have summer reading reports to write—I've been putting them off because I've been concentrating on my rodent olfactory experiments, but I'll stop by later if I can," he said before ducking back inside.

"What did he say?" I asked. "Ol-what-do-you-call-it experiments?"

Anna Marie looked down at me. "Old Factory experiments. He's supersmart!"

Anthony pulled his thumb out of his mouth. "Yeah,

and he has a *ginormous* maze in his room for his mouse, Pip!" he added. "He built it all by himself 'cause his mom lets him use a hammer—nails, too! That's 'cause he goes to a gift-wrapped school." He took a lick of the ice pop, and the top broke off the stick. It fell to the ground, splattering across my sandals.

Gram laughed. "Raphael will be a sixth grader at a *gifted and talented* school—one we'll be visiting tomorrow so you can take the admission test. It's a very prestigious school with extremely small class sizes—and best of all, free tuition. Anyway," she said as she wagged a finger up at the twins, "I know for a fact your mother wouldn't want you two leaning out the window that way, so get inside. I bought some lollipops yesterday; why don't you come down after supper. I'm sure *Magnolia* would love to hand them out."

Anna Marie squealed and clapped her hands. Purple droplets fell down on me as she yanked her brother back away from the window. I heard a loud thump, and Anna Marie shut the window, muffling Anthony's screams.

Gram chuckled as she put a key in the front door. "They are too much!"

I frowned, wondering how it was that Gram could smile and laugh at those loud, sticky kids when I didn't even rate a hug. I shook the grape slush off my foot and wiped my cheek. I'd have to make another wish because it was clear that *nothing* magical was going to happen anytime soon.

"Here's where you'll be staying," Gram said as I followed her down a long, narrow hall.

We stepped into a small room with light gray walls and a twin bed stuck in the corner by the window. One solitary painting of a sailboat on a stormy sea hung on the otherwise bare walls, and my heart sank. "This was Dad's room? Did he like boats?"

Gram peered at the picture. "Not exactly. I got that at a yard sale last week. I thought it might brighten the place up a bit."

I stared at the gray sky in the picture. It practically blended in with the walls. I'd hoped Gram would've kept a lot of Dad's old stuff. It would have been fun to see what he'd been like when he was a kid. I'd thought at least being with his things could make me feel more at home, but there was nothing homey about this small, dismal room.

"Your boxes are over there by the closet. Why don't you get unpacked?"

"Can I put up some of my posters?"

Gram gazed around at the blank walls. "That'd leave

holes in the walls." She turned to me and must've noticed how miserable I looked, because she quickly nodded her head. "I guess they won't be too noticeable. Well, I'm going to peel some potatoes for dinner. Your mother sent me her recipe—she said mashed potatoes are your favorite food, so I thought I'd give it a go."

"Thanks," I said quietly as she left.

I closed the door and walked around my new room. I counted twelve steps from the door to the window. My room in Colorado was probably more than double the size. It was no wonder Dad had told me to pack lightly.

I glared at the painting of the gloomy ship sailing against a gloomier sky. "I *wish* the sky was blue—with a rainbow."

Instantly the picture took on the feel of a tropical paradise. I smiled, thinking I should magic away the gray walls, but I knew that would be far more noticeable than the painting's makeover.

I walked over to my boxes and pulled out the tall, skinny one labeled POSTERS. Gram had left a pair of scissors on the desk near the closet, but I decided to have some fun unpacking.

"I *wish* the box would open."

Suddenly the tape on all seven of my boxes vanished, and the boxes collapsed in a heap. I rolled my eyes as books slid out, underwear and shirts tumbled down, and my shoes thumped to the floor. I quickly started putting things away before Gram would come in and see the mess.

Not wanting to take a chance having something go wrong with sharp thumbtacks, I pinned the posters up the old-fashioned way, and then I opened the tiny closet to put my shoes away. A couple of pillows sat on the shelf in the back, and I pulled them out so I could sit up and read later.

As I did, a piece of paper slid out from underneath the pillows and drifted to the floor. It was a drawing of a blond-haired boy holding a wand with yellow zigzags of lightning shooting out of the tip toward a pile of what looked like gold and jewels towering over the cartoon figure. Michael, my father's name, was written across the bottom in sloppy purple letters.

I brought the picture over to my new bed and sat down. I traced the zigzag lightning with my fingers, and my heart raced. Was the picture just a coincidence or . . .

I shook my head. My father was many things, but magical wasn't one of them. If he were, he certainly wouldn't have botched dozens of home repairs over the years that had required stitches and an assortment of carpenters, plumbers, and electricians rushing over for emergency house calls.

Dad was a scientist—serious and boring. He read biographies and scientific journals, and he lived for documentaries about things like the life cycle of a dung beetle.

I put the picture down and pulled the desk chair over to the closet. I stood up and saw a small pile of drawings toward the back of the shelf. Stepping down with them, I pulled the chair back to the desk and sat.

The first picture was of a woman levitating over a table as the blond boy waved a magic wand with the familiar bolts of lightning zapping out of it. Another had the boy sitting on a beach under a tropical, aqua blue sky—like the one now hanging on the wall—and a pod of dolphins at the water's edge. "Hi, Michael" was written in bubbles coming out of the dolphins' mouths. The next showed the boy standing by a large birthday cake and dozens of gift-wrapped boxes surrounded by more yellow zigzags.

The next piece of paper wasn't a drawing at all. It was a yellowed newspaper page. I unfolded it and saw a picture of two men standing on either side of a boy who couldn't have been more than two or three years old. The caption read: "McGuire and Malloy move to a new Bridgeport location."

I looked at the storefront pictured behind them and gasped. Clear as day was a big sign over the door: MCGUIRE & MALLOY'S MAGIC REPAIR SHOP. I looked at the top of the page to see the date and read "Fall Issue, Society for Ethical Magicians New England News, 1966."

My hands shook as I gazed back at the photo. The boy was obviously my dad, and I recognized Grandpa Malloy from the one family photo Dad had hanging in his home office. The other man wore thick glasses and had dark suspenders pulled tightly over a small potbellied stomach. The street sign on the left side of the photo was a little out of focus and in the fold of the paper. I could make out the first four letters—BARN—but the rest were unreadable.

Gram lived on Barn Swallow Boulevard, but I hadn't noticed any stores like the one in the picture when we'd driven up in the taxi. My eyes traced the magic repair shop sign over and over. Was it possible my grandfather had owned a *magic* repair shop? Could he do magic too?

I looked at the three figures standing in front of the shop. If my grandfather were a *real* magician, surely Dad would have mentioned it. Unless it was a secret—like *my* magic.

"Magic Repair Shop," I whispered. "How would someone *repair* magic?"

I pushed the chair away from the desk and headed for the kitchen with the newspaper page. "Gram!" I called out. "Look what I found!"

3

The Black Rock School
for the ~~Abnormally~~ Gifted
and Talented

The next morning, Gram and I got into a taxi to go to the Black Rock School's open house. I thought the ride over would be the perfect time to ask her more about the magic repair shop.

I'd tried to talk to her about it the night before, but she'd just waved her hand in the air like she was shooing away a fly, and said the shop was nothing but an old five-and-dime store full of "hokey magic tricks and gag gifts" nobody needed or wanted. Then she'd taken the clipping from my hand, ripped it in half, and tossed the pieces in the garbage on top of the potato peels.

When I'd gone to bed later, I couldn't stop thinking about that shop. If it was just a big nothing, why did Gram keep changing the subject every time I brought it up?

Around midnight I got up and fished the ripped-up newspaper out of the garbage and taped the photo back together. The picture—stained by the potato peels—was harder to see now, but I tucked it away in my desk so I could look at it in the light of day.

As the taxi went through an intersection, I shifted in my seat to face Gram better. "So, how does someone *repair* magic?"

Gram took a deep breath and then let it out slowly. "You're not going to let this go, are you? Your grandfather and Mr. McGuire repaired top hats that rabbits had chewed through and replaced broken switches on the cheap plastic wands they sold." She took her book out of her oversize handbag and opened it up where the bookmark was.

"But what exactly is the Society of Etha-something Magicians?"

Gram put the book in her lap and squeezed her eyes shut for second. "A group of men practicing card tricks and sleight of hand as an excuse to get out of the house."

"But they had their own newsletter."

"Oh, well." Gram paused, looking flustered. "Some of

them were serious about practicing their tricks I suppose, but—but I don't see why you're so *fixated* on all of this."

"Why didn't Dad ever mention the shop before? He told me Grandpa was a barber."

"Your grandfather quit the repair shop when your father was still little—he probably doesn't even remember it." Gram sat up straight and looked me in the eye. "It wasn't a good time for our family when your grandfather was working there. I do *not* want you bothering your father about all of this nonsense! *Is that clear?*"

"It's clear." I slunk down in my seat and caught Gram giving me a sideways look. "If this is the end of your interrogation . . ." She reached into her bag and pulled out the small vocabulary book she'd tried to get me to read yesterday after supper. "I suggest you concentrate on preparing yourself for your entrance exam. If you don't score high enough on the test, you'll be going to South Side Elementary, which, as I told you, was the site of numerous air quality problems this past year."

When the taxi finally pulled up to the school, I saw that it was in a much nicer area than the neighborhoods we'd driven through for the majority of the way over. Everywhere else there had been houses and apartments and empty storefronts crammed together—but here there were wide green lawns edged with flowerbeds, and I could see sailboats cruising on Long Island Sound. There was a pretty brick path leading up to the front entrance of the school, and a banner welcoming new students hung between two large marble columns.

Gram and I walked through the door, and a woman wearing a pink business suit rose up from behind a table and rushed over to us. She bugged her eyes out and flashed her bright white teeth. "I'm Delilah Davenport, president of the PTA, Extracurricular Activities Committee, Science Fair judging panel, and the Country Values Club—so happy to meet you!"

Gram held out her hand. "I'm Margery Malloy. This is my granddaughter, Maggie. She's here to take the placement exam."

After Mrs. Davenport shook Gram's hand, she looked me up and down. Her smile faltered a bit. "How nice. What grade are you going into, Maggie?"

"Sixth."

Mrs. Davenport clapped her hands together. "Oh, you *must* meet my daughter, Darcy. She's running for the sixth-grade class president." She leaned in closer to us. "It'll be her sixth consecutive year in office, you know. Now,

Maggie, why don't you run over to the activities table and introduce yourself while I give your grandmother some paperwork to fill out."

She pointed down the hall to a table littered with trophies and ribbons. "Don't forget to get a campaign button!"

"Okay."

I looked at the walls as I made my way to the table, thinking the school had gone a little overboard with the inspirational posters.

ONLY THE BEST AT BLACK ROCK! DARE TO REACH FOR THE STARS! REFUSE TO BE ANYTHING LESS THAN YOUR BEST!

A nervous tickle made its way up my spine. My grades were pretty good, but I got the feeling an occasional B or C would be frowned upon here. And what about my incident with Roxie? Gram had said that alumni sponsors who sent donations to cover tuition only cared about the test. But was I capable of scoring high enough to convince someone to sponsor me?

"I'm Darcy Davenport, may I be of assistance?"

I jumped and realized I was standing in front of the activities table. A small, pale girl with frizzy blond hair and a million freckles sat staring at me expectantly with piercing green eyes. There were science fair trophies, writing awards, math ribbons, and 4-H medals—and they all had the name "Darcy Davenport" printed on them.

"Hi, I'm Maggie. I'm here to take the admission test."

The girl continued staring at me. "Why?"

"Huh?" I said, wishing she'd blink or something.

"Why do you want to come *here*?"

I shrugged. "Because my Gram said it was the best school," I tried.

Darcy shook her head and fingered a large ruby set in a gold locket hanging from her neck. "You don't look driven enough to want this place." She stared up at me again and squinted. "There's no bloodlust in your eyes."

"Bloodlust?" I murmured, wishing she'd stop gawking at me. I also didn't like that she was implying I wasn't Black Rock material—especially since I had just been worrying about that very thing.

I thought about Raphael and the way he had smiled at me, and decided I wasn't going to let some crazy over-achiever intimidate me. "I met someone who goes here. He didn't have bloodlust in his eyes."

Darcy folded her arms across her chest. "Who was it? I know *everyone*."

"Raphael Santos."

She snorted. "Raphael Santos—the *Nutcracker*?"

"Huh?" I said again.

Darcy held her wrist out and touched a button on an oversize watch. "I'll give you five seconds to figure it out."

My mind scrambled. Raphael? Nutcracker? Walnuts? Christmas? Rodent olfactory experiments?

"The Mouse King!" I said, smirking. "From *The Nutcracker* ballet."

"Correct." She smirked back at me. "But it took you *seven* seconds."

My smile disappeared. "Why wouldn't you just call him the Mouse King?"

She rolled her eyes. "We did, but he *liked* it too much. He's *obsessed* with mice." Darcy sighed. "Look, here's the deal. This school is made up of a combination of future Mensa candidates and genius slackers."

"Mensa?" I asked.

Darcy rolled her eyes again. "It's an organization for people whose IQ is in the top two percent of the population—like mine."

I groaned inside. Darcy had clearly already decided I didn't fit into either group.

"Anyway," she continued, "Raphael is definitely in the slacker category. All he cares about are his pseudo-scientific experiments with his stupid mice. He isn't even working on anything that he could write a paper on to submit to the school's science journal. Seriously, *olfactory processes*—how kindergarten is that?"

"The school has its own science journal?"

She raised her eyebrows. "They didn't have one where you came from?"

"Maggie!" Gram called, waving me back over to her.

"Um, it was nice to meet you," I lied. "Hopefully I'll see you in class."

Darcy nodded, but the sneer on her face told me she thought otherwise.

"Wait," Darcy called out. "I'm running for class president. Take a button—*just in case.*"

I took the pink VOTE FOR DARCY button and felt bad for the unfortunate person who might be running against her. I had a feeling Darcy Davenport would run a mean campaign.

Darcy sat up straight and folded her arms on the table. "Oh, I don't want to brag, but we have to take an admission test every year . . . and I scored higher than any of the returning students in my class. I had *six* alumni offers to sponsor me." She folded her hands on the table, looking wide-eyed and innocent. "Good luck."

My shoulders slumped as I walked toward Gram. I squeezed my fists, wincing as the pin on the back of

Darcy's button poked into my hand. I was smart, but I knew my IQ wasn't in the top two percent of the country, and it was going to take more than luck to get in.

I also knew a little magic might just help me set a new admission test record and take Darcy Davenport down a notch.

4

Reykjavik!

"Okay, Maggie." Mrs. Davenport plastered a smile on her face. "I'll be taking you and Fiona to the sixth-grade testing room."

A sullen girl with long brown braids sat on a chair with her knees pulled up to her chest.

Mrs. Davenport tapped the toe of one of her high heels on the floor a few times and then cleared her throat. "*Ms. Fitzgerald*, it's time. *Again*."

Fiona dropped her feet to the floor. "I'm ready," she said, getting up slowly.

Gram reached out and put a hand on my arm. "Don't rush. And double-check your answers!"

I nodded, following Mrs. Davenport and a droopy-looking Fiona into a room with only eight desks.

"Maggie, why don't you sit in the back, and Fiona, you can take a seat in the first row. I'll get the tests from the office safe and then we can begin."

As soon as Mrs. Davenport left, Fiona stretched her arms above her head. She turned to me and sighed. "This is my sixth time taking the admission test. My older sisters—all three of them—go here. My parents have spent *a lot* of money on tutors to help me, and if I don't pass this test, I'll be in huge trouble."

"Maybe sixth time's the charm," I said, thinking I should work a little magic for Fiona, too. "What're the tests like?"

Fiona grimaced. "According to my sisters, they're so easy, even an idiot could pass them. I don't know what that makes me, but I have zero memory for the names of obscure islands off the coast of Africa. And don't get me started on the personal essays. A thousand words about what law I think a historical figure would propose to Congress and why?" She rolled her eyes. "Apparently my idea that P. T. Barnum would support a law for the ethical treatment of circus animals failed to impress the headmaster last year, but a lot of people don't realize how badly the animals are treated."

Barnum! Had that been the name of the street in the newspaper clipping? "Is there a Barnum Street or something in Bridgeport?" I asked suddenly.

"There's a Barnum Avenue. Why?"

"There's a place I want to visit there," I said. "If it's still there, that is. Do you know where—"

Mrs. Davenport came in with a folder in her hand and stood in the front of the room. "Are we ready, ladies?" She slipped the tests out and gave one to each of us. "As you already know, Fiona, the first part is a multiple-choice test covering reading, vocabulary, science, and math. Fill in each circle completely, and if you want to change an answer, make sure you erase your mark thoroughly."

She patted a machine on the desk. "When you're done, we'll just scan your tests here and get the results. The second part is a personal essay. There are two topics to pick from. Choose carefully." She smiled brightly. "Because there is only one opening for grade six."

Fiona looked back at me. I thought she might start to cry.

"You'll have two hours to complete both parts. Good luck."

I bit my lip. I'd planned on making a wish to help us both ace the tests, but with only one slot I wasn't sure what to do. I opened my booklet and read the first question.

What is the capital of Iceland?

A. Baranovichi

B. København

C. Reykjavik

D. Vaduz

I looked at the choices. Not only was I clueless about what the answer was, but I didn't even know how to pronounce most of the names. Geography was never my best subject, so I flipped to the science section. I scanned the questions. I knew a lot of the answers, but I wasn't going to beat Darcy without help.

And what about Fiona? I nibbled on the pencil eraser, looking up to see Mrs. Davenport reading a magazine at the front desk.

I worked out what I wanted to say, checked to see that Mrs. Davenport was still reading, and whispered, "I *wish* Fiona would score higher on the test than Darcy did."

I figured that was a nice, straightforward wish not likely to cause anyone to lose their hair or make a chimpanzee materialize in the room.

My lips curled up in a sly smile. It would be kind of funny to see Mrs. Davenport's reaction to Barty Bananas.

I peeked at Fiona and saw her sit up straight and then

start furiously filling in the circles on her answer sheet.

It was a sure thing Fiona would finally get in, but where did that leave me?

What if I wished for another opening in the sixth grade? If I was going to start using my magic, why not try for something big?

"I *wish* Fiona and I would *both* score higher than Darcy *and* that we would both get into the school."

I took a deep breath and wondered how my wish would play out. My stomach fluttered nervously. What if my wish caused someone to get hurt, or worse? What if a bus hit some kid just so I could get in?

My heart pounded. Why hadn't I thought this through?

"I *wish* no one would get hurt or die because of my wish!" I whispered quickly.

"Did you have a question, Maggie?" Mrs. Davenport asked.

I looked up. She was staring at me with one pointy, plucked eyebrow raised. "No," I squeaked out. "I was just, uh, talking to myself."

She raised her other eyebrow. "Well, try to keep it down, dear—we wouldn't want to disrupt Fiona's concentration."

Fiona was still scribbling at lightning speed, and I

figured I'd better get going too. I turned back to the first page and looked at the answers for number one again. "Reykjavik"! I filled in the circle on the answer sheet and smiled.

The timer rang and Mrs. Davenport shut her magazine. "Pencils down, please!" Apparently she hadn't noticed that Fiona and I had finished ages ago.

The door opened and a short man wearing a bright yellow tie came in. He waved to Fiona and then walked over to me. "I'm Mr. Petrie, headmaster of the Black Rock School. How did the exam go, ladies?" he asked.

I nodded. "Fine, sir."

Fiona beamed. "I think I did really well this time!"

Mrs. Davenport gave Fiona a sympathetic smile as she walked around the desk to collect her test. "I'm sure you did."

"It certainly would be nice for you to be able to join your sisters this year," Mr. Petrie added. "And an extra slot just opened up in your grade."

My heart skipped a beat.

"Oh?" Mrs. Davenport said, looking very interested.

"Wendell Skinner's parents have decided to homeschool

him so he can devote more time to his language studies." Mr. Petrie looked at Fiona and me. "Wendell is something of a prodigy when it comes to languages, and he'll be traveling overseas with his parents so he can work on some different dialects."

"Wow, that's great," I said, enormously relieved that my wish was sending Wendell Skinner to Europe and not the hospital.

"Well, let's see how you did on the multiple choice," Mr. Petrie said. He took the tests from Mrs. Davenport and walked over to the test scorer on the desk. "Ms. Fitzgerald first." He fed the answer sheet into a slot and the machine clicked and whirred for a bit. The paper came back up and Mr. Petrie whistled.

"One hundred percent!" Mr. Petrie said slowly. He turned to Fiona and shook her hand. "This is *outstanding!* We've only had two children with perfect scores in the twelve years I've been headmaster. I'm looking forward to reading your essay, but this pretty much guarantees you a spot."

Fiona and Mrs. Davenport both looked like they were going to faint.

"I've got to tell my mom!" Fiona squealed as she raced out of the room.

"Now, Ms. Malloy, I don't want you to worry—no

one is expecting you to get a hundred too." He inserted my test and I crossed my fingers. He took it out and gasped. "Why, this is unheard of."

He showed the test to Mrs. Davenport and her mouth dropped open.

"There must be something wrong with the machine," she said. "We'll have to hand-grade these."

"Is something the matter?" I asked.

"It seems you've scored a hundred percent as well," Mr. Petrie said, appearing a bit dazed.

"How is it possible?" Mrs. Davenport asked.

"I don't know," Mr. Petrie said. "But just wait until we put out an e-mail—the alumni will be fighting over who gets to sponsor these students."

"Excuse me," I said, my heart racing. "Does this mean I got in?"

Mr. Petrie nodded. "It certainly does! Welcome to the Black Rock School, Ms. Malloy."

"B-but wait," Mrs. Davenport sputtered. "We really should look at their essays, just in case—"

Mr. Petrie waved the test in Mrs. Davenport's face. "Delilah, no one will give a fig about the essays when they see perfect scores on these tests." He turned to me with red-tinged cheeks. "What I *meant* to say was that your essay on how William Shakespeare would address global warming is sure to be a fascinating read, but there's no way we can turn you down with this score."

He tilted his head toward the door. "Why don't you tell your grandmother the good news?"

I did it, I thought, feeling giddy as I walked down the hall. And I helped Fiona too! I felt unstoppable—like a superhero.

I chewed on my lip. It was sheer luck that Wendell Skinner wasn't hurt—I'd have to be careful. But the new me was off and running—and itching to make a lot more wishes!

5

Lost and Found

"Wow," Raphael said as we sat on the front stoop of the apartment building later that day. "A hundred percent? That's unbelievable!"

"I know!" I said gleefully.

"The freaky thing is," Raphael continued, "it's, like, statistically impossible both of you would get a perfect score. Off the top of my head, I'd say you'd have a greater chance of dying from a venomous snakebite, and that's one in 3,441,325!"

He stared at me with his big brown eyes—half hidden under a mess of brown curls—and the superhero feeling faded rapidly away.

I suddenly realized it was going to take a whole lot of wishes to make sure Fiona and I kept up with our new classmates. And off the top of *my* head, I'd say I had a fifty-fifty chance of making a magical mess with a wish-gone-wrong that would get me expelled yet again.

"Well, someone's got to beat the odds, right?" I said nervously.

Raphael nodded. "Whatever the odds, I'm one hundred percent positive that Darcy Davenport will have a fit when she finds out. Wait till you meet her. She's like this evil genius who *really* enjoys being number one. You might think about doing some major sucking up, or she could make things rough for you."

I stared at Raphael. "Rough?"

He leaned in closer to me, talking in a low voice as if Darcy might be lurking nearby. "In third grade Nahla Jackson did a science fair experiment with hydroponic vegetables, and our teacher was so impressed, she called a scientist from Yale University to come see it. Darcy was beside herself that Nahla's project was getting more attention than hers. But the day of the fair, all the water mysteriously dried up and Nahla's plants were attacked by dozens of hornworm caterpillars and aphids—and this was in the middle of the winter!"

"Let me guess, Darcy wound up winning."

"Yup, and the scientist alerted the newspaper about Darcy's last-minute surprise entry on the discovery of a new comet. She got written up in five periodicals. I'm sure you saw her on the cover of *Amateur Astronomy*."

I sighed. In third grade I was playing with plastic ponies while Raphael was reading *Amateur Astronomy* magazine—along with probably every other kid at Black Rock. I was in way over my head. "Yeah, um, my parents must've let my subscription expire. But I'm pretty sure Darcy's already heard about my test score. She was at the school today, and her mother administered the sixth-grade test."

Raphael smiled gleefully and rubbed his hands together. "Well, at least we won't have to listen to her brag about her score for another year."

Raphael hunched his shoulders, narrowed his eyes, and lifted his scrunched-up nose in the air. *"I was thinking,"* he said in a high-pitched squeaky voice, *"that the temperature will reach the nineties today, which just so happens to coincide with my placement test score. And I think the cafeteria will be serving mini turkey burgers, which each contain approximately ninety-five calories— which coincidentally was my score last year."*

Raphael laughed at his own imitation as my stomach sank. I was definitely in for it. Between risky wishes and the wrath of Darcy Davenport, sixth grade was sure to be more trouble than a crazed chimp tossing birthday cake around.

I decided it was time to change the subject. "Do you know where Barnum Avenue is?" I asked Raphael. With Gram working at the local food pantry, and only two days before Black Rock's opening day, I figured this was the perfect time to do some investigating and take my mind off school troubles.

Raphael's brown curls bounced as he shook his head up and down. "It's just a couple of blocks from here. Why?"

I shuffled my sneakers in the grit on the sidewalk. "My grandfather used to work in a shop there. I was just wondering if it's still around."

"Well, it's a big street—roughly three point seven miles if I had to guess. The section near us is mostly closed-up stores and abandoned apartments. What's the shop called?"

"McGuire and Malloy's Magic Repair Shop," I said.

"*Magic* repair shop?" Raphael laughed, and I realized how ridiculous it sounded.

My cheeks reddened. "My grandmother said it was some kind of joke shop, but I have an old picture of it. I just wondered if it was still around."

The squeal of tires rounding the corner made me

jump. My eyes popped as a purple stretch limousine with the words MILO THE MAGNIFICENT plastered along the side streaked past us and screeched to a stop at the corner. The back window was covered with a picture of a mustached magician—the same one on the posters I'd seen—waving a wand with a trail of stars streaming out.

The driver's door opened, and a humongous man lurched out of the car. He had to be almost seven feet tall, but he wasn't skinny like a basketball player—he was more like three-hundred-pounds-of-Bigfoot tall. He walked over to the back door, but as he was reaching for the handle, the window rolled down. Milo leaned out and slapped the driver's hand away.

"What are you doing, you illiterate buffoon?" Milo shouted. "McGuire's is on Barnum *Avenue*, so why in Houdini's name are you stopping on *Barn Swallow Lane*?"

I sat up straight on the step as the large man looked up, squinted at the street sign, and pursed his lips. "Barnum?" he finally said, giving Milo a puzzled look.

"Yes, Barnum, you hulking gorilla! Now get back behind the wheel this instant!" Milo hollered. "Find the repair shop so I can get this rabbit under control before tonight's show!"

The chauffeur lumbered back to the driver's door, and in a flash the limo streaked down the street, kicking up a cloud of dust and dirt from the sun-baked asphalt.

Raphael and I exchanged wide-eyed looks. I knew in my gut that my wish had *finally* come true! Something magical was really about to happen.

"Hey," Raphael said. "That was the guy who's on all the magic show posters. Weird, huh?"

"No," I whispered. "Not weird, *magical!*" I jumped up, and without thinking, started to race down the block in the direction the limo was going.

"Maggie?" Raphael called after me.

I heard footsteps pounding on the sidewalk, and then he ran up alongside me. "Where are we going?"

"We're following that car," I said breathlessly.

M y sides ached as we sprinted toward the limo that had just parked in front of a boarded-up building. I fought to catch my breath as I looked at the other closed-up storefronts lining the block. "It's got to be here," I whispered.

"Hey, look!" Raphael said.

He pointed toward the ground, and I finally saw it—a neon sign above a stairwell leading down to a basement shop. It was smaller than the sign I'd seen in the newspaper photo, and even though some of the letters were dark, it clearly said MCGUIRE AND MALLOY'S MAGIC REPAIR SHOP.

"Raphael, that's it!"

We headed across the street just as the chauffeur reached a monster-sized hand for the back door. Milo the Magnificent, wearing a dark purple cape over a lavender tuxedo, popped out onto the sidewalk.

"Where is it?" Milo shrieked, his eyes darting around wildly as a dozen or so white rabbits hopped out of the car around his feet.

"Wow, look at all of them." I laughed as the rabbits started nibbling on the tufts of grass poking through the cracks in the sidewalk.

Milo placed his hands on his hips. "Are you sure you followed the directions . . ." He took a step forward and tripped on a rabbit. His ankles wobbled, and the driver reached out and yanked his cape to keep him from falling. Milo put a hand to his throat, gagged, and then slapped the driver away. "Get off me, you lumbering oaf!" he coughed. "Just find the blasted shop!"

"It's there," I called out. "Right down those stairs."

Milo looked at the shop sign and then turned to his chauffeur. "Reginald! Throw these infernal creatures in the satchel with the others! And you there," he said, wrinkling his nose as if Raphael and I smelled like the moldy cheese Gram liked to eat, "stop staring like simpletons and grab some of these rodents!" He turned on his heels and marched toward the stairs.

My first thought was, *Who the heck do you think you are, ordering us around?* But the next was, *Here is what seems like an honest-to-goodness, real live magician looking for grandfather's old shop!* If I wanted to know what was really going on down there, this was my chance. I grabbed the nearest rabbit, held it tightly in my arms, and followed after him.

Milo was already at the bottom of the stairs, kicking the door with the tip of his pointy black boots. "McGuire!" he yelled. "Open up!"

A shadow crossed the dark store window, and then the small front display lit up, illuminating a toy rabbit sticking out of a dust-covered black top hat. I heard some keys rattling and the door opened.

Milo pushed past an old man and started ranting. "Someone—obviously consumed with jealousy—cast a spell. My rehearsal was ruined by a rampaging horde of replicating rabbits! There were at least a dozen of them— hopping off into the orchestra pit, biting my assistant, *pooping* on the stage! And more keep appearing. If you don't do something quickly, we'll be drowning in rabbits."

The door shut, muffling his voice, and I hugged the bunny tighter in my arms. Did he say someone had *cast a spell*? Was it too much to hope that there was real magic inside this shop and not just gag gifts and tricks like Gram had said?

"Excuse me, miss," said a deep, rumbling voice that made the hairs on the back of my neck stand on end. "Do you need help?"

I turned to see the chauffeur, Reginald, directly behind me. I stared up into his empty, gray eyes and shivered. The dead fish on ice at the grocery store looked more alive.

"Uh, no, I'm okay," I finally mumbled.

Reginald nodded and heaved a squirming bag over his shoulders, clomping down toward the door.

The rabbit I was holding wriggled in my arms. I held it fast and looked down, shocked to see I was now holding two! Butterflies fluttered in my stomach as Milo's words echoed in my head. Had a rabbit just magically *replicated* itself in my arms? "Raphael!"

I turned back and saw Raphael staring at four rabbits sniffing the sidewalk at his feet. He looked up at me with a wrinkled brow.

"Maggie," he whispered. "I was going to pick up these two rabbits and all of a sudden there were four. I think I need to go lie down."

I beamed at him. "No, it's okay. Didn't you hear what he said? The rabbits are multiplying. It's magic—that's why he brought them to a *magic* repair shop!" I felt as though I was going to burst from excitement.

Raphael's eyes grew wide. He shook his head and gave a crazy little laugh. "Ha, yeah, but that's not how rabbits multiply. They need a mommy and a daddy rabbit."

"It's *okay*, trust me. Let's just go down to the shop."

Raphael paled and he looked like he might get sick. "I don't think we should go down there, Maggie."

I suddenly realized how scary duplicating rabbits must be for someone like Raphael. There was no scientific theory explaining how one rabbit could turn into two with a blink of an eye. Or how cockroaches could magically appear in a girl's hair.

I knew that wishes coming true wasn't something covered in any textbook that Raphael had read, but in my heart I knew I'd find answers in that shop. "Look, you can stay up here or you can go home, Raphael, but I'm going in. I have to."

Raphael's eyes turned to the shop sign and he took a deep breath. "But it's, it's impossible . . ." He looked down at the rabbits milling at his feet and shook his head. "It can't be."

"Nothing's impossible, and if you go with me, maybe you'll learn something that they don't teach at the Black Rock School."

6

Hide-and-Seek

Raphael and I managed to get through the door of the shop without dropping any rabbits, and we placed them on the floor with at least thirty others roaming around.

Once my eyes adjusted to the dim light inside, I saw that the walls of the shop were packed with books and jars filled with bright powders and sparkling liquids. A lemon-yellow cat blinked its eyes as it stretched on a shelf above canisters labeled with things like "freeze-dried ogre lice" and "pickled chicken feet."

"Wow," Raphael whispered.

The hair on my arms stood up as electricity seemed

to build in the air. Suddenly red and purple sparks shot out from the tips of a dozen wands standing in a silver container, sending the cat scrambling off the shelves and into the back room.

"Wow," I echoed.

I turned in a circle and took the room in, gaping at shelves that didn't hold boxes of bloody rubber fingers or plastic vomit like I'd seen in other "magic" shops. This was the real deal, and my grandfather had *worked* here. Gram *had* to know what was really going on in this shop. So why had she lied? And what about my dad?

Raphael elbowed me and pointed to Reginald, who was standing in a corner staring straight ahead, seemingly unaware of what was going on around him. I counted to eleven before he blinked.

The sack of rabbits lay open at his feet, and I was about to ask Raphael if we should try to corral them, when the old man who had opened the shop door pushed through a set curtain behind the counter.

He was wearing stained brown pants held up by red suspenders that stretched tight across his generous belly. He had a clipboard tucked under his chubby chin and was carefully carrying a tank filled with the largest, wartiest frogs I'd ever seen.

"Don't walk away from me, McGuire!" Milo said,

brushing the curtains aside as he shadowed the old man's steps.

My first thought was that Mr. McGuire certainly didn't look like a real magician—not like Milo did. Of course, with my sunburned nose and messy blond hair, I wasn't sure how magical I was looking either. But I couldn't help wondering if a real magician wouldn't use some sort of spell to keep his pants up instead of being seen in public with suspenders.

"I demand you help me *immediately*, McGuire!" Milo continued, stalking around to the front of the counter.

Mr. McGuire put the tank down and snapped his suspenders. He caught my eye and a quizzical expression crossed his face. "I really must attend to these frogs," he said to Milo.

"Frogs? Are you serious?" Milo asked. "Apparently you haven't been paying attention. The rabbits have chewed my best hat and wand, eaten through four boxes of magic dust, and bitten six of my assistant's fingers! I have my first show this evening, and I won't let these blasted hares make a fool of me. You're the magic repairman—do something!"

Mr. McGuire sighed. "It appears someone's cast a level four duplicating spell on your original rabbit. Duplicating spells are not to be taken lightly. And," he added, "I'm sure you've heard about the magicians who've vanished over the summer."

Mr. McGuire turned and pointed to three flyers hanging behind the counter. The first two showed men dressed in fancy top hats and capes. The third pictured a young woman wearing a diamond tiara with doves flying from her open hands. The same words appeared at the top of each flyer:

HAVE YOU SEEN THIS MAGICIAN?

CALL

The Society for Ethical Magicians

1-800-55MAGIC

"I'd be a bit concerned if I were you," Mr. McGuire continued. He opened the lid on the tank, grabbed a frog, and dunked it into a bowl of pink liquid. "Do you know anyone capable of casting a spell of that magnitude who you've perhaps rubbed the wrong way?"

Milo straightened up and clutched the big purple brooch at the neck of his cape. "The wrong way? I am *loved* by everyone. Just fix the problem! I have a performance in four hours and I won't have these multiplying menaces interfering."

An angry red flush crept over Mr. McGuire's face. "I wish I could help you right away, but as I said, there've been all sorts of magical breakdowns lately." He picked up the clipboard and showed him a paper with "TO DO" written in black marker across the top. "I have an obscure hex to break, several wands to fix, and these frogs to de-wart. Not to mention a black cat turned yellow, doves laying lumpy eggs, a cauldron that's burping flies, and an enchanted painting to debug."

Raphael scurried to my side. "Magical breakdowns? Hexes?" he whispered incredulously. "Are they crazy or is this the most amazing discovery since scientists figured out how to unravel the DNA of a woolly mammoth?"

"They're not crazy," I whispered back. "Check out all the bunnies; what more proof do you need?"

Milo removed his cape and started picking rabbit fur off the purple velvet, making it clear that he was staying put. "One would think a repairman with too much work would hire an assistant."

Without giving it a second thought, I said, "I think I could help you."

Raphael turned to me with his mouth open.

I walked up to the counter and held out my hand. "Mr. McGuire, I'm Maggie Malloy, and I think my grandfather used to work with you. I'm staying in

Bridgeport with my grandmother, and I would love to help you here in the shop," I said breathlessly.

Mr. McGuire stared at me as he shook my hand up and down. "Maggie *Malloy*? Could it be?"

I nodded. "I found a newspaper clipping in my dad's old room—it was a picture of you and my grandfather in front of the repair shop in 1966."

"Yes! That was our very first place. I've downsized since then, but . . . my, my—I can see a lot of your father in you." His eyes watered up. "I must say, this is a most unexpected surprise!"

"And opportune," Milo interjected. "I suggest you employ the girl immediately so that you can attend to my problem."

Mr. McGuire looked back and forth between Milo and me. "Oh, I don't know. Not to say I don't appreciate the offer, Maggie, but you're a little young to be working in a magic repair shop. And then there's your grandmother. I have a feeling she wouldn't be crazy about the idea."

"You're in no position to be turning down offers of assistance, if you ask me," Milo said. "This shop is about to be overrun with replicating rabbits."

Mr. McGuire placed his glasses on his big nose and blinked at the crowd of rabbits gnawing on his shelves and books. "Oh, my," he said, snapping his suspenders.

"They do seem to be duplicating at a truly astonishing rate."

Please, I silently begged.

Mr. McGuire smiled. "Well, I suppose I could use some help finding Milo's original rabbit. I can't imagine your grandmother could object to that."

I looked around at the sea of white rabbits and my shoulders slumped. "There must be nearly a hundred of them now, and they all look the same."

"If you've got what it takes, you'll be able to find the original," Mr. McGuire said.

"Egad!" cried Milo, rolling his eyes.

"I *can* find it!" I said, determined to show Milo the Magnificent I was every bit as magical as he was.

Raphael waved a hand in the air. "I want to help too."

Milo twitched his nose.

"Well . . . ," Mr. McGuire started.

"I may be just a kid," Raphael said, looking serious, "but by my best estimates, if these rabbits keep multiplying at this rate, there'll be over a thousand before the hour is up. Multiply that number by all those sharp teeth and claws, and I think you need all the help you can get."

It was then that an idea struck. "Don't worry, Raphael, I've got this covered." I smiled sweetly at Milo and said, "I *wish* the real rabbit would appear."

I scanned the room, waiting for one of the rabbits to hop over, or glow, or even do some sort of silly dance, but they just kept milling around chewing on things. I looked up at Milo staring at me with his top hat clutched in his hands, and my stomach did a nervous flip.

"*Maggie,*" Raphael said out of the corner of his mouth. "Don't just stand there. Start looking." He waved a hand at the rabbits, urging me on.

"I *wish* the *original* rabbit would appear," I whispered.

When nothing happened, I knelt and gently picked up a rabbit, praying some sixth-sense thing would kick in and let me know if I had the right one. But as far as I could tell, he was just an ordinary bunny. "One down, ninety-nine to go," I muttered.

I put the rabbit in my lap and held it down with one hand, then grabbed another. Okay, I thought, comparing the rabbits side by side. Same white fur, same gray eyes, and—I leaned over and gave the rabbits a sniff—same dusty smell.

The rabbits hopped to the floor, and I brushed away the fur that was stuck to my nose. "Well, one of these bunnies has got to be different, right?" I mumbled, feeling my heart race.

Raphael knelt down beside me. "Let me help." He picked up a rabbit and held it up to Milo. "Do you recognize this one?"

Milo groaned.

Raphael scrunched up his forehead and gave his head a good scratch. "This is going to be harder than I thought."

Milo stared at Raphael for a second and then turned to Mr. McGuire. "Is this really necessary? Must I stand here for an eternity while these urchins fumble around? Surely there is a spell you can use?"

Raphael sat up straight and nodded at Milo with wide eyes. "Now, *that* is something I'd pay to see. Can you guys actually . . . you know . . . do *that*?"

"No!" I yelled. "I said I'd find it and I will." I snatched up a fourth rabbit and yelped as it dug its long nails into my neck and wiggled out of my arms. I looked out at the carpet of white fur, feeling hopeless. Was there some *trick* to figuring it out? They were all the same. And more of them kept appearing. How could I even be sure which ones I'd checked?

Mr. McGuire shook his head. Mouth pursed, brow furrowed, he looked as disappointed as I felt.

I bit my lip, trying to stop the tears pooling in my eyes. I'd dreamed about meeting people like Milo and Mr. McGuire, but this wasn't the welcome to the world of magic I'd imagined. This was a test—and I was failing it.

"Well, are we ready to move on?" Milo asked. "It was

rather preposterous to expect this child to do the work of a seasoned magician."

I shot one of Gram's looks at Milo. "I'll find it!" Then I noticed his eyes. He had the same gray eyes as his chauffeur. Not quite the same, though. His were sharper. He caught my stare and turned away, pulling his top hat down on his forehead.

Suddenly I knew.

"There!" I cried, jumping up. "It's in your hat!"

7

Hasenpfeffer

"Now, see here!" Milo said, taking a step back. "I think I would know if I had a rabbit in my hat!"

"It's in there, I know it—I couldn't find it before because it was hiding!"

"Did you have your hat off in your car?" Mr. McGuire asked. "Could the rabbit have gotten in?"

Milo wrinkled his nose and sniffed. "I suppose it's possible the coward could have snuck in during the ride over," he said slowly. "But really, it seems highly unlikely—"

"You suggested I give Maggie a job," Mr. McGuire said. "If she thinks the rabbit is in there, let her look."

Milo snorted as he took his hat off and handed it to me.

I peered into the dark opening and my heart sank. It was empty—absolutely empty.

"Do you see anything?" Raphael asked.

I tilted the hat toward him, feeling a wave of overwhelming disappointment wash over me.

"Oh," Raphael said quietly.

"Not so fast," Mr. McGuire said. "Give it three taps, right on the rim."

I tapped three times with my fingers, and suddenly the hat felt heavier. "There's something in it!" I put the hat on the counter and Raphael raced to my side. I reached in and gasped as my arm went in all the way to my shoulder. Fishing my hand around, I was amazed to feel a stream of warm air circling my arm. Finally my fingers brushed against several pairs of rabbit ears!

I gently lifted the first bunny out by the scruff of its neck.

"You found it!" Raphael cried.

"Nope," I said, handing him the bunny. "This isn't the one." I reached in again and pulled out another one. I held it up to the light, and buried my face in its soft fur, feeling its heart beating against my cheek.

"This is it, Mr. McGuire!" I yelled, happy tears filling my eyes. "There's more in there, but this is the one."

Milo's mouth curled into a sneer. "How can you be sure?"

"It just is," I said. "It's different. Its fur smells like hay, not dusty like the others. And look," I said, holding the rabbit up to Milo, "its eyes—they're pink! All of the others are gray."

Mr. McGuire took the rabbit from my arms, gave it a once-over, and smiled like I'd just given him a million dollars. "I knew it! I just knew it! You've got it! The minute I met you, I *knew*. Your father must be so proud of you."

Suddenly a loud beeping went off and Raphael fumbled through his pockets until he pulled out a cell phone. "Oh no, I forgot about my bagpipe lesson!" He flipped the phone open and grimaced as shouts blared out. "I'm sorry, Mom, I'm just around the corner. I'll be right home." As he shut the phone, his face screwed up with disappointment. "I have to go, but . . ." He looked all around the shop as if he needed to take everything in one more time, and then he dashed for the door. "But you have to tell me absolutely everything when you get back!"

I turned to Mr. McGuire as the door slammed. "Why didn't anyone tell me about my grandfather? I've been hiding my magic all these years, because I thought I was some kind of freak. Why didn't they tell me?"

Mr. McGuire snapped his suspenders nervously. "You didn't know? Oh, well—um. It was a long time ago, and well . . ." Mr. McGuire paused. He wrinkled his brow as if he was trying very hard to remember something.

"Well, your grandmother never did think the magic repair business was suitable for a family man. But your grandfather would be proud that you are carrying on the old family ways."

Mr. McGuire turned and wiped his eyes with his bandanna as I tried to figure out how it was possible no one thought to mention the fact that magic runs in the family!

"Excuse me," Milo said, knocking his knuckles on the counter. "This is all very touching, but perhaps you can reminisce when we're not so besieged with bunnies!"

Mr. McGuire nodded. "Yes, of course, you're right. Maggie's found the original rabbit, so it looks like I—I mean, *we* can help you after all."

Mr. McGuire clucked his tongue as he examined the list of ingredients in an old, worn spell book. "I have everything we need right on the shelves," he said to me. "The jars are in alphabetical order—well, they were. I've gotten a bit sloppy over the years, I'm afraid, but hopefully we'll find what we need without too much fuss."

Milo jabbed his watch with a pointy finger. "Tick, tock, McGuire!"

Mr. McGuire took a deep breath and forced a smile on his face. "It's not a complicated spell, so it should go quickly. Your patience is greatly appreciated."

Mr. McGuire turned to me and rolled his eyes as he placed a small glass bowl on the counter. "First up, I'll need the jar labeled MD number four off the shelf behind the counter."

"MD number four?" I asked.

"Magic dust number four. It's a fine green powder."

I found the jar and handed it to Mr. McGuire. He carefully measured two teaspoons and poured them into the bowl. "This will help bind the ingredients together. Now I need a jar labeled 'Origins.' It helps things get back to their original state."

I walked along the shelves, tracing my fingers along the jars and canisters. "Oak moss, obsidian, ogre lice, okapi hair, opossum tails, ostrich feathers—*origins!*" I pulled the jar of what looked like shimmering blue dust off the shelf and blinked as the contents started to glow.

Mr. McGuire unscrewed the lid, and a beam of light shot out of the jar. "It's harvested from fallen stars created during the origin of the universe." He poured the stardust out into a measuring cup and added it to the bowl, where it continued to radiate.

After Mr. McGuire gathered some more ingredients,

he checked the spell book one last time and used a step-stool to reach a box.

I looked at the label in surprise. "Freeze-dried carrots?"

He winked. "Just a little something extra to ensure the spell is a success."

He crumbled a wilted-looking carrot into the bowl and then took an old white-tipped wand from beneath the counter. The black enamel paint was worn in spots, but when he tapped it on the edge of the bowl, a silver spark shot out from the end. "It's seen better days, but it still packs a punch," he said.

He waved the wand over the bowl. *Too many rabbits running the shop, mix it all up so they'll stop the hop.*

The powders rose up out of the bowl in a swirling cone as if they were being sucked up in a mini-tornado. He flicked the wand toward the bowl, and the ingredients dropped back down in an evenly speckled mix.

"Okay, the last thing we need is the mirror. Maggie, please go in the storage room behind the counter and wheel out the large mirror with the blue sheet over it. Be sure to keep the sheet on, though," Mr. McGuire warned. "It's imperative it stays covered!"

I waded carefully through the rabbits toward the back room. Milo let out a loud "humph" and started pacing, sending bunnies scurrying from the tips of his boots.

"Perhaps you could help clear a path," Mr. McGuire said, "so Maggie can wheel the mirror out?" I turned back and smiled at Mr. McGuire—liking how he wasn't taking any of Milo's nonsense.

Milo waved a hand in the air toward his driver. "Reginald! Move these creatures out of the way!"

Reginald blinked twice, then shuffled forward. I shuddered as I pushed the curtain aside, hoping he wouldn't squash any bunnies under his Bigfoot-size feet.

The back room was filled with more books and boxes and mostly empty cages. A few doves flapped their wings and cooed when I walked past. I saw the mirror and ran my fingers down the blue silky fabric embroidered with all sorts yellow swirls and crescent moons. I lifted a corner of the cover, wondering what could possibly happen if I just took a little peek. A strong, wet wind smelling of rotting fish roared out from under the sheet and whipped around my head. I jumped back and the sheet fell flat.

"Maggie, do you need help?" Mr. McGuire said.

"Tick! Tock!" Milo added.

"Coming," I called, my heart pounding as I brushed my hair back in place. *Keep the sheet on.* I leaned into the mirror, and the wooden wheels turned with a squeak.

As I pushed the mirror out into the main room,

Mr. McGuire picked up the mixing bowl and made his way over to it. "Place Milo's hat on its side so the opening will show in the mirror's reflection," he said. "Then put the original rabbit in the hat."

I put the hat in front of the mirror, then opened the cage we'd put the rabbit in for safekeeping. "What about these two?" I asked, pointing to the gray-eyed bunnies sitting with the original.

"Put the duplicates on the floor with the others," Mr. McGuire said.

"There isn't much room left," I said, gently pushing rabbits aside to make space for the new ones. "Now you." I lifted out the original bunny and smiled at his pink eyes. "No more multiplying." I shooed him into the hat and stood up.

Mr. McGuire took a deep breath. He ripped the sheet off the mirror and threw the powder onto the glass.

A bright light flashed toward the hat on the floor, and all of the duplicate rabbits sat up on their haunches and stared at the mirror. They slowly leaned forward—noses twitching—and then suddenly started scrambling over one another in a race to get to the mirror.

Waves of purple and orange light flared out from the mirror as each rabbit leapt into the hat's reflection.

Within minutes they'd all jumped in, disappearing

through the glass until only the original rabbit remained snoozing in Milo's hat.

Mr. McGuire covered the mirror and wiped his brow with his red bandanna. "Ta da!" he said with a flourish of his hands.

"That was the coolest thing I've ever seen!" I squealed. "Could my grandfather do stuff like that? Can *I*?"

"Jerry could have done just about anything he wanted. He was a very powerful magician, much stronger than I." Mr. McGuire took my hands and smiled. "And it's obvious you've got magic dust running through your veins too."

My heart began to pound. I glanced over at Milo. He was staring at me, and I wondered why he wasn't rushing off to his stupid show.

I faced Mr. McGuire, and even though I didn't want Milo to hear me, after all these years I couldn't wait another second either. "I wish for things. I wish for things and they appear. I didn't know how I could do it, or where the stuff came from—and I learned to be really careful about what I wished for," I said, my voice getting louder, the words rushing out. "I even had to practice not saying the word 'wish'! But when I did, it was just for little things like sodas mostly, because I ran into trouble when I accidentally wished up this monkey, Barty Bananas, from—"

"Oh," Reginald called out, startling me. He covered his mouth with his hands and giggled like a little kid. "Barty Bananas is a funny monkey! I love it when he throws banana peels and the elephants and lions slip on them."

I stared at Reginald. He beamed at me, nodded his head up and down, and then his face went completely blank again.

"Uh, yeah, well, he wasn't so funny throwing cake around the room," I said, surprised Reginald was a Barty Bananas fan, "but sometimes my wishes don't come out exactly like I thought they would."

Mr. McGuire nodded. "Wish magic can be very inexact."

"I'm just so relieved to finally find out I'm not the only one in my family who can do magic!"

"Let's try something." Mr. McGuire walked over to a rolling ladder and climbed to the top rung. He reached for a jar filled with smooth, clear rocks and lowered it to me. "Open it," he said, climbing down.

I scrunched my nose as I struggled with the lid. "I *wish* it would open." The top moved smoothly and I twisted it off. Mr. McGuire reached inside and flinched as he grabbed one of the rocks. I sucked in a breath as the rock began to sparkle in his hands, flashing blue, then red, purple, and finally a continuous yellow light crackled and glowed.

"Take one," he said. "You may feel a bit of a jolt."

I reached in for a stone and jumped as a shock traveled up my arm to the top of my head, making my hair flutter. My eyes widened as the rock turned from blue to red, then purple, yellow, black, and orange—ultimately ending with an intense white light.

"My, my, my. This is *fascinating*," Milo said. He looked me up and down. "I guess appearances can be deceiving. She doesn't have anything on me, of course, but she certainly shows you up, eh, McGuire?"

"What does he mean?" I asked as the stone stopped glowing.

"These stones act as a meter of sorts, a crude measure of magical power, if you will," Mr. McGuire said. "Magicians at the lowest level will cause the meter stones to turn blue. Few magicians get to purple, let alone white." He turned to Milo. "On the rare occasions I've seen the stones go past white, they delivered quite a nasty punch. You see," he said looking at me, "the more magical you are, the bigger the shock you get when you pick it up."

Milo looked at his watch and frowned. "This is all very enthralling, but I really must be going. I'm always interested in new talent, though. I'm sure I'll be running into you again, Margaret."

"It's Maggie."

"Yes, yes, of course. *Maggie*. I'll be very sure to remember that." Milo bent over and dumped the rabbit out of his hat before placing it on his head. "Might I purchase one of those rocks, McGuire? It might prove to be an amusing toy."

"Certainly," Mr. McGuire said. "I'll add it to your bill."

"No need to write up a bill." Milo walked to the counter and threw an envelope down. "This should more than cover your services."

He reached his hand toward the jar but pulled it back at the last second. I was disappointed because I'd been looking forward to seeing him get a really good zap.

"Reginald, gather my new purchase. And be quick about it! We really must get to the theater."

Milo was at the door when I noticed his rabbit nibbling on the bottom of the counter. "Hey, wait!" I called, picking it up. "What about him? Don't you need him for your act?"

Milo turned and sniffed the air. "What I do is not an 'act.' It is an exhibition of finely honed feats of magic that showcase my prodigious ability." He pointed his nose down at the rabbit and sniffed again. "As for that repellent rodent, I won't have him sullying my reputation. You can use him for hasenpfeffer for all I care!"

Well, I'd had it with Milo. It wasn't the rabbit's fault someone had cast a duplicating spell and wrecked Milo's rehearsal. And I didn't know what *hasenpfeffer* was, but I could tell it wasn't anything a rabbit would appreciate being a part of. So I did something stupid. I made a wish.

I bent my head down, pretending I was hugging the rabbit, and I whispered into one of its ears. Smiling at Milo, I gave him a wide-eyed, innocent look. "Well, I'm sure you'll be much better off without him," I said, trying not to laugh. "It's just too bad the heat curled your mustache." I made a spiral in the air with a finger. "You *really* ought to fix that before the *big* show."

Milo ran his fingers over his upper lip and pulled at the tight corkscrew mustache under his nose. Eyes blazing, he huffed out of the shop with Reginald hulking along at his heels.

I felt triumphant—loving the start of the new me—but then my stomach flip-flopped when I saw Mr. McGuire staring at me with his hands on his hips.

"Hasenpfeffer?" I asked—hoping he hadn't noticed the makeover I had given Milo's mustache.

"It's a German dish. Rabbit stew."

"Ew." I headed for the cage and away from Mr. McGuire's disapproving look. "Don't you worry, little fellow, we won't be serving hasenpfeffer anytime soon!" I put the rabbit in and shut the latch, trying to think of something else to say.

"While I don't condone what you did, Maggie, I thought the curls softened what, in my opinion, is a rather stereotypical look for a stage magician."

I laughed, but my cheeks burned. "I'm sorry, I shouldn't have done that."

"You're right, you shouldn't have," he said sternly.

I looked down at my sneakers, figuring my career in the magic repair business was over before it had even started.

"Because," he continued, "it's never a good idea making enemies of powerful magicians—no matter how deserving of a little hex they might be. Not that your grandfather ever took my advice. He once increased a customer's receding hairline by two inches while the man argued over a bill."

I tried to contain my smile. "I really am sorry."

"Let's just try to remember the customer is always right. Not necessarily nice, but always right."

Mr. McGuire walked over to the counter and opened the envelope Milo had had left.

I gaped at the huge wad of one hundred dollar bills. "Wow!"

"Milo must've been feeling generous. This is above and beyond what I'd charge for a case like this." He put the money in the register and then put his hand on the rabbit's cage. "I guess I'll put our new guest out back for now. I have a friend coming over tomorrow who might be persuaded to take it."

"Could I keep him?" I asked. "I could call him Hasen-pfeffer. Maybe the name will keep him out of trouble, and he'd be a souvenir from the first magic repair job I helped with." I poked my fingers through the bars and rubbed his head between his ears.

"I'm quite certain I'll be in the doghouse with your grandmother for this, but I happen to be of the opinion that every budding magician needs a rabbit."

"Does this mean you'll let me continue to help out in the shop?" I asked hopefully.

Mr. McGuire pursed his lips. "It would be nice to have some company down here, but I don't know."

"What if Gram says it's okay?"

He clucked his tongue. "If she gives her approval, and that's a big if—" He smiled. "You could help me in exchange for magic lessons."

Visions of spells and transformations swirled in my head. I felt like I had finally found a place where I fit in. "Do you mean it? You'll teach me how to cast spells and—"

Mr. McGuire held up his hand. "Let's not get ahead of ourselves now. Using your magic to wish for sodas is not the same as casting spells."

"But I'm ready! You saw the stone. I can do it. I—"

Mr. McGuire kept his palm up and I held my breath. "There's a lot of ground to cover before I put a spell book in your hands. Magic can be complicated. There are rules, and not following them can get you in a whole lot of trouble. Plus, business comes first. You'd be working here because I do need the help."

Mr. McGuire opened the small tank on the counter and picked up a large frog covered with knobby lumps. "What do you know about de-warting frogs?"

8

Wishes
and Nightmares

"Work in the repair shop? Absolutely not!" Gram said later that day. She turned to Mr. McGuire with wide, angry eyes. I wouldn't have been a bit surprised if bolts of lightning had zapped them and singed off what little hair he had left on his head.

"It's bad enough you told her about her grandfather," she said, shaking a finger in his face like he was a child. "Goodness knows the ideas you've put in her head, and then you let her bring that creature up here—it's already escaped from its cage and chewed through a lamp cord!"

I couldn't for the life of me figure out what Gram was all upset about. My grandfather had worked in the shop! And the way Mr. McGuire was stammering made it clear he was as confused as I was. I was really glad we hadn't told her yet just how much I had in common with my grandfather.

"Oh, well, really, Margery, I just assumed she knew about Jerry—I assumed she'd been told."

"Well, she hadn't, and if you spent any time away from that shop, you'd know there's a whole world out there that exists perfectly well without magic!"

Mr. McGuire fidgeted with his suspenders. "I am terribly sorry. I never would have said a word if I'd known."

Gram looked at me and scowled. "I should've known you'd go poking around after you found that newspaper clipping."

"Why didn't you want me to know?"

Gram folded her arms across her chest. "I have my reasons."

She and I stared at each other for a second, and Mr. McGuire cleared his throat. "It's just a small rabbit," he said quietly, holding his hands a few inches apart.

"That rabbit is the least of my concerns. Maggie could get hurt, or worse. It's not all parlor tricks and sleight of hand, you know," she said, looking down at me.

"I've witnessed some things that would give a young girl like you nightmares, and I"—she took a deep breath—"I don't think it's any place for a child."

"Things aren't like they were in the old days," Mr. McGuire said. "I'll just have her dusting and sorting, and maybe mixing a few things up for me. I won't take her on any outside jobs, and I'll keep her away from the more, uh, complicated things. It would be nice to have some regular company down there again."

"This whole discussion is pointless," Gram said. "School starts up the day after tomorrow, and Maggie will be swamped with assignments."

"What if I only go after all of my homework is finished?"

Her brow furrowed, and I could almost see the excuses swirling in her head as she tried to come up with more reasons to keep me from the shop.

"What if I only go on weekends and days off to start with, so I don't get behind?" The Black Rock School started two days before Labor Day weekend. If she agreed to it, I'd have tomorrow in the shop, just two days of school, and then three whole uninterrupted days of magic!

She shook her head. "It's an extremely competitive school, Maggie. It wouldn't hurt to throw yourself into your work and get ahead."

I started to worry that Gram wasn't going to change her mind.

She took the glasses from her pointy nose and rubbed her eyes. "But maybe taking the weekend off isn't such a bad idea," she said as she chewed the brownish lipstick off her lips. She put her glasses back on her nose and waved a hand toward a window. "You haven't explored the city yet. There are dozens of things to do that would be far more interesting than hanging around in a gloomy, old shop."

I stared at Mr. McGuire, silently pleading with him to say something.

"Margery, really, she'll be fine."

Gram put her hands on her bony hips, looking more determined than ever to find a way to keep me out of the shop. She wasn't going to give in.

I gave Mr. McGuire a sneaky sideways glance and bit my lip. "Gram, please, I really want to do this. I *wish* you'd reconsider."

"I'll handle this!" Mr. McGuire cut in, and boy, did he shoot me a look.

My cheeks burned.

"Now, Margery, we've been friends for forty years. How can you think I'd put your granddaughter in harm's way? I promise, she'll just help out with the little things.

I really could use a hand, and it's just wands and animals I'm busy with."

"Oh, you two." Gram scrunched her mouth into an angry pucker. "It's just that your . . . well, never mind. I suppose it's really not my decision to make. I'll leave it up to your parents, Maggie. They'll be calling tonight before they head into the rain forest. If they say it's all right, I guess I'll have to go along. But don't get your hopes up—I plan on telling them exactly what I think of the whole idea."

I was so happy, I wrapped my arms around Gram's tiny waist, not caring that she hated to be hugged. "Thank you, thank you, Gram. You don't know how much this means to me!"

"Don't get excited yet." She gently pushed my arms away, then brushed at her shirt as if my hug had left her covered with dust. "Now off to your room, young lady. Mr. McGuire and I have some things to discuss."

I lay in bed trying to listen to Gram and Mr. McGuire, but the rumbling cars in the distance made it impossible to hear much of anything.

I leaned over, reached my hand into Hasenpfeffer's cage, and rubbed his ears. "They have to say yes," I whispered. "*Nothing* is going to stop me from working in that shop!"

I got up and went to the window. I closed my eyes and shut out the city. I pictured my parents seven years ago—my dad with his beard, my mom with that bright red hair color she had tried out. I pictured the balloon tied to the desk chair, and the birthday cake with five candles dripping yellow wax on pink frosting. I took a deep breath and made a new wish, hoping this time it would come out just right.

"I *wish* you'd forget. I *wish* you'd forget that monkey ever existed. I *wish* you'd forget that day existed. Please—forget."

I took a deep breath and exhaled slowly. I opened my eyes and stared down at the insects beating themselves against the streetlight until my heart slowed and my hands stopped shaking.

I looked at my new pet defensively. "I didn't have a choice. It's better to be sure they don't remember." I smiled. "I should have done that a long time ago."

I bent down and scooped up a handful of shavings that Hasenpfeffer had kicked out onto the rug. "Better be careful," I said. "Gram's not real happy you're here, and she's just the kind of person who *would* put you in a stew if you're too messy."

Hasenpfeffer sneezed and crawled under his blanket.

"Too bad you can't talk—I'll bet you've seen some really cool stuff."

I hopped back into bed, but there were too many things running through my mind to even think about sleeping. Why hadn't anyone ever told me about Grandpa? And my dad—he hardly ever even talked about Grandpa. Nothing made sense. Could Dad have grown up without knowing his father was a magician? Did Gram tell him the same thing she had told me—that it was just a joke shop?

I thought about Mr. McGuire. While we had been de-warting the frogs, he had told me about some of the repair jobs he'd done over the years. Simple ones like magicians' assistants who wouldn't stop levitating, and decks of cards that bit their owner's fingers with tooth-less mouths. And scary ones too—like volunteers who disappeared into boxes and couldn't be summoned back.

The strangest story had been about a woman named Viola Klemp who had been sawed in two by a new magi-cian, the Amazing Armando—an amateur who Mr. McGuire had said shouldn't have been practicing magic at a professional level. No matter how hard Armando had tried, he hadn't been able to get Viola's two halves reattached. The spell had been botched so badly, it had taken Mr. McGuire and my grandfather four whole days to figure out how to put Viola back together.

"Luckily, Viola was a good sport about the whole incident," Mr. McGuire had said. "The only thing she was really worried about was that Armando would have the chance to do this to someone else.

"Your grandfather and I made sure his performing license was revoked, but he was so shaken by the whole thing, I don't think he would have tried that trick again! The incident inspired Viola to start a watch group to keep an eye on incompetent magicians. They've become quite powerful over the years—they even manage licensing now in the U.S."

I yawned and rubbed my eyes. Maybe Gram was right about the magic business being dangerous. I dragged my fingers across my belly and shivered at the thought of being sawed in half.

When I finally drifted off to sleep, I dreamed I was back in the repair shop. It was filled with rabbits again, and I picked one up to see if it had pink eyes.

"Little girls mustn't mess with magic," the rabbit whispered, its voice sounding exactly like Milo's. I dropped it and started toward the mirror, struggling in a sea of rabbits now up to my knees. When I finally reached the mirror and ripped off the blue sheet covering it, rabbits began to leap out of the mirror, filling the shop with Milo's voice. "Little girls mustn't mess with magic. Little girls mustn't mess with magic."

"I *wish* you'd all disappear!" I screamed, but more and more rabbits jumped out and began scratching and clawing at my arms and legs as they fought for room to move.

I woke suddenly, covered in sweat. The clock's glowing numbers said it was just after eleven. As the blood pulsing in my ears quieted down, I heard Gram talking on the phone and jumped out of bed.

I opened the door and Gram shook her head. "You might as well hear it from them," she said, handing me the phone.

"Hello?" I said in a shaking voice.

"Maggie!" my dad boomed. "So glad we caught you before we head out into the jungle. You'll never believe this, but Dr. JoŸson says the team we're taking over for found a new species of cockroach yesterday—your mom and I will be among the first people to see it!"

"Wow, new cockroach, lucky you," I said. "So, uh, Gram talked to you about me working in that . . . shop?"

"Well, your grandmother thinks you're a little young, but your mom and I think it sounds like the perfect way to learn some responsibility. Nothing like sweeping floors and scrubbing toilets to help you appreciate all the work we do around the house. But your schoolwork comes first. Speaking of which, congratulations on getting into the Black Rock School. I knew you were smart, kiddo, but wow!"

I noticed Gram frowning and suppressed a smile. "Don't worry, homework will come first."

"That's my girl! And I hear you've acquired a rabbit."

"I named him Hasenpfeffer."

I heard Dad repeat the name to Mom, and they both laughed. As much as I was happy about meeting Mr. McGuire and discovering the repair shop, hearing them laugh together on the other side of the world—without me—brought prickly tears to my eyes.

"Hasenpfeffer! That's a good one," Dad said. "Oh, hold on—your mom wants to talk."

My mom started in about the new cockroach, but I barely heard the rest of the conversation. I pushed out all thoughts of missing them and concentrated on going down to the shop in the morning and finding out what my first magic repair job would be.

9

Milo's Gift

The next morning, I lay in bed counting down the minutes until the repair shop would open.

I leaned over the edge of the bed and tapped on the rabbit cage. Hasenpfeffer looked up and sniffed my fingers. "Good morning!" I said. "I just thought you'd want to know that I am the new assistant to the great Gregory McGuire, magic repairman extraordinaire."

He blinked his pink eyes and yawned.

"Well, I thought it was exciting news. And you'll be happy to know my parents said you could come home with me when I go back to Colorado—unless, of course, you want to go back to Milo the Meatball?"

Hasenpfeffer jumped, kicking a mess of shavings out onto the rug. "For pity's sake," he cried out, "do you want me dead?"

I stared at Hasenpfeffer, unable to speak. I blinked twice and pinched myself to see if I was still dreaming.

"Well?" he asked. "Do you? Of course, we rabbits are at the mercy of humans. Really, it's a wonder I'm still alive, what with all the—"

"You can talk!" I interrupted.

"Oh, for pity's sake." He hopped over toward the cage door, sat up, and squinted at me. "You don't appear to be stupid, but we've been conversing for at least a minute now, so it's abundantly clear I can talk." He tilted his head and regarded me again. "You *do* know you cast the spell that made my speech possible?"

"I didn't cast any spells."

Hasenpfeffer lay down and stretched out his rear legs behind him. "Tsk!" he said, burying his nose under the edge of his blanket. "Everyone knows magic rabbits are highly susceptible to suggestion, and last night you said, 'Too bad you can't talk.' It was right after you magically erased your parents' memory."

I grimaced and felt the flush on my face deepen.

Hasenpfeffer peered up at me from beneath the blanket and shook his head. "Apparently you're not only woefully ignorant about rabbits, but you've got questionable morals as well. Frankly, I wonder if I would be better off with Milo."

"But I was just afraid my parents wouldn't let me work in the shop!"

"Oh, that makes it perfectly fine, then. Let me be the first to congratulate you. You've taken your first steps toward becoming an evil magician—what's on your schedule for tomorrow—making magic money to buy whatever it is preteen girls just *have* to have?"

"You don't understand!"

Just then Gram rapped on my door. "Maggie, it's almost time for me to leave!"

"Okay, Gram." I turned to Hasenpfeffer. "Look," I said in a hushed voice, "you'd better keep quiet around my grandmother."

"Why? What's she got against rabbits? We're cute, easy to care for, although I must insist we sit down and discuss this cage—it's highly inadequate for my needs and—"

"Let me put it this way," I said, getting down low so I could look Hasenpfeffer in the eye. "Gram isn't a big fan of magic—or rabbits—and if she hears you talking, I can guarantee you'll be out on the street."

Hasenpfeffer turned and crawled under his blanket. "What kind of a person doesn't like rabbits?"

"A person who got their lamp cord bitten through."

"But I was bored. I used to be a world traveler. Now I'm stuck staring at a rather horrendous pink unicorn poster."

"Hey, that's one of my favorites." I turned and looked at the pastel unicorn prancing through a meadow of neon-colored flowers.

Hasenpfeffer sniffed in the direction of the poster. "I stand by my original assessment."

"Fine." I folded my hands across my chest. "I *wish* the unicorn would be replaced by a rabbit."

A giant pink rabbit appeared on the poster, and Hasenpfeffer made a mad chattering sound. "That is just unnatural!" he complained.

"So is a talking rabbit. Now, if you'll excuse me, I have to get ready for work."

As I headed down the hall, I hoped Gram would be in a better mood this morning. I went into the kitchen, where she was washing out her coffeepot. "Good morning," I said, trying to sound cheerful.

Gram turned off the water and dumped the pot so

roughly in the drying rack, I was surprised it didn't break. "I've been up all night thinking about this job of yours, and I've got a few things to say before you head down to that shop, young lady."

I sighed. If anything, her mood had taken a turn for the worse.

"You do exactly what Mr. McGuire tells you." She dried her soapy hands on a dish towel, pausing as if she wasn't sure what she wanted to say. "And if anything unusual happens, or anything seems strange, I want you to come right back here. I mean it! Working down there may seem like fun, but—well, just be careful. Magic is real, and it isn't something little girls ought to be messing around with."

I shuddered, thinking about my nightmare. I wanted to tell Gram about my dream, but I knew she'd just get more upset and probably keep me from going altogether. I forced a smile. "Don't worry, Gram, Mr. McGuire is a pro. *Nothing* will happen."

"It's not Gregory I'm worried about." Gram slumped her shoulders. "Maggie, I'm sure you're confused about all of this, but that shop caused a lot of heartache." Tears welled up in Gram's eyes. "I know you're not your father . . ."

Gram looked away and sighed. "We'll talk about it later," she said softly. She picked up her keys and turned back, seeming once again like her usual self. "I've got to get to the food pantry to help sort the new shipment. They really wouldn't know what to do if I wasn't there to direct things. I'll be back by four o'clock at the very latest. Gregory has the number, and there's juice in the fridge and bagels in the breadbox. I left some turkey for lunch, or there's ham if you prefer. And remember—after today, school is your number-one priority!"

She gave me a quick pat on the arm and headed out of the apartment, leaving me baffled. I shook my head, gulped down a glass of juice, grabbed my key, and opened the door to leave. There in the hall was Raphael.

"Hey, Maggie, I was just gonna knock. Do you want to spend our last day of freedom at the shop? I went there after my lesson, but you'd already left. Mr. McGuire told me how he got rid of the rabbits. It sounded so cool! I wish I could've seen it. Did you know he has a box of real leprechaun gold? And when I went back, he was fixing a painting of a dachshund that wouldn't stop barking bad words. But I thought up like a zillion new questions to ask him—I mean, everything I've always thought and believed has been completely turned around, you know?"

I nodded. "Actually, I was just on my way there, but . . ."

A black mouse poked its head out of the front bib

pocket of the overalls he was wearing. I jumped back and knocked my head on the doorframe. "Ow!"

Raphael picked the mouse up and held it out to me. "This is Pip. She's been kind of depressed since her sister, Squeak, died, so I decided to take her to Mr. McGuire's. I thought maybe there's a spell or something that can cheer her up."

Pip sat up on her hind legs and sniffed the air. As much as cheering her up sounded nice, I kind of wanted to go to the repair shop alone. I had a million questions I wanted answered too.

"Actually, Mr. McGuire hired me as his new assistant. I probably shouldn't bring my friends to work with me— it's not very professional. So, I'd better get going." I locked the door, walked past him, and started down the hall.

"Wait," Raphael said. "I can help too."

I sighed. "Look, Mr. McGuire hired *me* because . . . I'm a magician."

"A *magician*?" Raphael raised one eyebrow. "*You* can do magic? Like Mr. McGuire? I know you pulled that rabbit out of the hat, but—"

"I happen to be a magician with a great deal of power—apparently. You should have seen this meter stone I held after you left. I'm even more powerful than Mr. McGuire!"

Raphael eyed me suspiciously. "Let's see you do something."

"Fine." I held out my hand. "I *wish* butterflies would appear.

Four black caterpillars materialized on my open palm.

Raphael stared at the caterpillars for a second and then gaped at me. "Whoa, you weren't kidding!" He bent his head down and looked closely at them. "Not exactly butterflies, but I guess they will be eventually."

My cheeks flushed. "I *wish* the caterpillars would turn into butterflies—*now!*"

The caterpillars rapidly grew and then spun silky cocoons.

"They're moths!" Raphael said. "Butterflies make chrysalises."

I'd seen enough moth cocoons in my parents' lab to know he was right. "Well, they're related to butterflies." The cocoons moved in my hands, and then four giant moths pulled themselves out. They pumped up their crumpled wings, showing off dark eyespots, and with a few beats they took off down the hallway.

"Wow," Raphael said with appreciation. "Instantaneous metamorphosis. Even if they weren't butterflies, that was still pretty cool!"

I smiled. "My wishes don't always work perfectly."

"So," Raphael said, "I guess I can tell you *my* secret, then."

"Secret?"

Raphael looked me up and down like he was sizing me up.

"You can tell me!"

"Okay, but you have to do the secret swear." He held Pip out to me. "Place your hand on Pip, and swear on your life that you won't tell a nonmagical person what I am about to tell you."

I wrinkled my nose. "You want me to swear on your mouse?"

"Mice are very intuitive, and Pip will know if you're trustworthy enough to hear the secret that *only* Mr. McGuire knows."

I took a deep breath and put my hand on Pip; I was surprised how soft her fur felt. "I swear on my life not to tell anyone." I took my hand away, and Pip sniffed it.

Raphael pulled Pip back and opened a front pocket for her to crawl into. "She didn't bite you, so you've passed the test." He looked around the hall a second and then leaned in close. "I come from a long line of magicians myself. My ancestors were exiled from Puerto Rico a hundred years ago after my great-great-great-great-grandfather turned the mayor's oldest daughter into a statue!"

My mouth dropped open. "He turned her into a statue? Why?"

Raphael narrowed his eyes. "'Cause he thought she'd make a great gargoyle to scare the pigeons away. I got kicked out of my old school for doing the same trick on this crabby lunch lady. They ended up making her into a fountain and put her on the front lawn. I hear the cafeteria food has never been better."

"Really?"

Raphael burst out laughing. "Oh, man, you should've seen your face!" He opened his mouth and bugged out his eyes. "Like anyone would make a fountain of someone wearing a hairnet."

I put my hands on my hips. "So that whole story was a lie?"

Raphael nodded. "For a magician with a great deal of power, you're pretty gullible."

"Well, *thanks* for the laugh, but if you don't mind, I have some *real* magical business to attend to! Have fun with your mouse." I started down the hall, feeling like an idiot for believing that stupid story, even if it was just for a second or two.

"Hey, it was just a joke," Raphael said, catching up to me. "But I'll come down to the shop and help out—even if I'm not a magician. Race you!" He picked up speed and I hustled after him.

"Wait!" I called out.

Raphael turned around, smiling. "Did you need me to give you a head start?"

"No! It's just that going down to the shop is really important to me. And maybe . . ." I paused. "Maybe it would be better if I went alone."

As soon as the words left my mouth, I wished I could take them back. Raphael's smile crumpled. "I may not be all *magical* like you, but Mr. McGuire said I was welcome to come back anytime I wanted."

"I'm sorry—everything's coming out all wrong!" I cried as Raphael reached out for the front door. "Just let me explain what happened yesterday."

Raphael ignored me and pushed open the door. "Hey!" he said as Milo the Magnificent brushed past him. "It's you, the magic guy!" Raphael followed Milo down the hall. "We met yesterday, remember? Well, I didn't get to introduce myself, what with the rabbits and all, but I'm Raphael Santos."

He held out his hand, but Milo just glared down at him as if he were a small bug he was about to crush with his pointy shoes. "The correct term is magician, not 'magic guy,'" he said coolly. "Now, if you don't mind, why don't you run along and do whatever it is little boys do."

Milo turned to me and smiled like we were best friends. "Maggie, you're just the person I was looking for.

How delightful to see you again!" Milo tipped his purple hat, then pulled the brim down low on his forehead. "I'm terribly sorry I had to run off yesterday, but you know how show business is," he said, waving a white-gloved hand in the air. "But now . . . I have more time to chat."

Goose bumps popped up all along my arms. The last thing I wanted was a "chat" with Milo! "We," I said, grabbing Raphael's arm, "were just going to Mr. McGuire's. We really don't have time to talk."

Raphael yanked his arm away. "We?"

"Actually, it was more of an offer of assistance I had in mind," Milo said, taking off his gloves. "Why doesn't your little playmate toddle off? You can catch up with him in a few minutes."

Raphael narrowed his eyes and curled up his lip. "Don't worry, you *magic guys* take all the time you want."

"I *wish* you wouldn't go, Raphael," I blurted out.

Raphael turned around, eyes blank and staring. "Um . . . okay," he said slowly. "I guess I, uh, can stay." He walked back and stood next to me with his forehead all scrunched up.

Milo sighed. "Very well, young man, I only wanted to give Maggie something, and I'll be on my way."

He held out his hand, and a small purple book suddenly appeared.

"*Magic for Beginners?*" I read aloud, my nose twitching from the rotten egg smell coming from it.

"A gift from me to you," Milo said. "It's just a fun little book. Maybe it will help you decide if a career on the stage is in your future. After all, it's good to know what you're getting yourself into. Magic doesn't always work the way you want it to. I can attest to that. And, who knows, you may find it isn't something you care for."

"Thanks," I said, reaching out to take the book. I shivered as my fingers brushed against his hand. "I'll take a look at it."

Milo nodded. "I always take great pleasure in helping those magicians less gifted than myself, and I believe this will give you a lot to think about. Well, I'll not keep you any longer, but perhaps we'll run into each other again." He tipped his hat, turned, and walked out the door.

Raphael and I watched Milo stride down to his limousine. Reginald lumbered out and opened the back door for him.

"That guy gives me a serious case of the creeps," I said.

"At least he gave you that book," Raphael said. "And look, he even wrote it."

I ran my finger over Milo's name embossed on the purple cover, then looked up at Raphael. "Hey, I'm really sorry about before. I was a total jerk."

I was trying hard to look sorry, but I could tell he wasn't totally convinced. "I really *wish* you'd forgive me."

Raphael's eyes softened and I grinned. This was too easy. "It's okay," he said.

I smiled. "So, um, I'm going to be pretty busy today and won't have time to read this book; do you want to borrow it? Maybe you can pick up some tricks."

Raphael's eyes widened and he snatched it out of my hand. "Maybe I *could* pick something up from this. I'm about as beginner as it gets, and statistically it wouldn't be impossible that I could have some repressed hidden powers just waiting to be unlocked." His eyes popped even wider. "That would be so cool!"

Raphael opened the book. I was pretty sure he wasn't going to be bugging me anymore today. "Thanks!" he said as he walked down the hall to the elevator, flipping pages. He looked up once to punch the elevator button, and when the doors opened, he walked in without saying good-bye.

"You're welcome," I whispered. A tingle of uneasiness crawled up my spine.

I shook my head. *Magic for Beginners?* How bad could it be? And it was highly doubtful he had actual hidden powers, I thought as I opened the front door.

The moths I'd conjured up flew out over my head, and I smiled. Not just anyone could be a magician.

10

Blisters and Boils

When I got to the stairs leading to the shop, I skipped down, threw open the door, and rushed inside. "Sorry I'm late, but—" I called out right as I slammed into someone wearing a dark, scratchy cloak. I sucked in my breath as my feet left the floor and I landed on top of our first customer of the day.

"Hey!" a woman's voice called out from under me.

I struggled to untangle myself from the wool cloak, wincing as the rough fabric rubbed against my skin. I stood up and held out my hand, then pulled it away, not sure if I should offer to help her up or not. "Oh, I'm so sorry," I said. "I was running, and I—"

"With the luck I've had, I should've seen it coming," the woman interrupted, slowly pushing herself up. She let out a long groan, and as she stood her hood fell away to reveal a mess of orange curls. She turned to me, and I stepped back—her face was completely covered with red sores oozing yellow pus.

"Oh!" I said, and then felt horrible, knowing I'd started off on the wrong foot with *another* customer. "I didn't mean to—I—"

"Don't sweat it, kid, at least you didn't scream. That's what I did when I looked in the mirror and saw I'd turned into a walking pizza." The woman smiled and held out a hand, which I was relieved to see was unblemished. "I'm Franny. You must be Maggie. Gregory told me all about you. He and your grandfather helped me get my business started many moons ago."

I shook her hand, trying not to stare.

"Pretty scary, huh? Too bad it's not Halloween. I'd win first prize." Franny laughed and gently blotted her face with a cloth.

"It's not that bad," I said, shaking my head.

"We've just met and you're lying to me already?"

I relaxed my shoulders and laughed. "All right, it's pretty bad."

Franny laughed with me, and I knew she was one of

those people who make you feel like you've known them for years, even though you've just met.

"But I wouldn't be so jovial if I didn't think Gregory could fix this mess," Franny said.

"Ah, Maggie, I see you've met the Bride of Franken-stein," Mr. McGuire said, carrying an armload of books from the back room. He placed them on the counter and studied Franny and me for a few seconds. "Should I assume that your disheveled appearances have something to do with the ruckus I heard out here?"

"As a matter of fact, they do," Franny said, straightening out her cloak. "She thought I was a monster and tackled me."

"Oh no! It was an accident. I didn't even see your face. I . . ." Franny started laughing again, and I realized she was kidding.

"Franny likes to tease," Mr. McGuire said. "Don't pay attention to half the things she says. Taking care of that ghoulish face of hers is the first order of the day, though." He walked over to Franny, pursed his lips, and shook his head. "I'd like to get my hands on the person who did this!"

"Someone did this to you?" I asked, eyes wide.

Franny nodded. "I was hexed."

"Hexed? Like a spell?"

"Basically they're the same. A hex is usually a bit meaner than your run-of-the-mill spell, though," Franny said.

"Tougher to repair, too," Mr. McGuire added. "I've tried several remedies already." He looked at Franny and clucked his tongue. "I really had high hopes for the tonic I made from skunk spray—something about the smell often helps dissolve tough spells."

I stared at Franny's blistering skin. "What kind of a person would do something like this?"

"A not-so-very-nice one." Franny sighed. She walked over to the counter and hopped up next to the stack of books. "I raise enchanted animals—you know, like rabbits and doves. I collect special breeds from all over the world for spells or magic acts."

"Certain breeds are more conducive to magic than others," Mr. McGuire said. "Franny supplies these special creatures to my shop and to most of the other places that sell magic paraphernalia."

"Some guy called a month or so ago trying to sell me enchanted rabbits," Franny said. "He said he could get me a steady supply—cheap. There is tremendous demand for first-class enchanted rabbits, but I like to do my own breeding. You wouldn't believe the Easter bunny rejects people try to pass off as magic. Anyway,

I told him I wasn't interested, but he wouldn't take no for an answer."

"Why didn't he just sell them himself?" I asked, leaning on the counter, running my fingers up and down the book spines.

"Nobody can raise enchanted animals like Franny can," Mr. McGuire said. "She has a special gift for it—that's her magic. I'm sure whoever had the rabbits knew he wouldn't be able to sell many of them himself."

"And I certainly was not about to buy rabbits from some nameless person!" Franny added with a snort. "He wanted to remain anonymous and send his 'associate' to deliver the rabbits. When he wouldn't let up, I threatened to turn him over to the Society for Ethical Magicians."

"That's the group that was started by the lady who was sawed in half, right?" I asked.

Franny nodded. "And you don't want to mess with Viola Klemp. Some people say she was born mean, but others say it was being sawed in half for days that added lemons to her personality."

"Don't listen to her, Maggie," Mr. McGuire said. "Viola is a lovely person—most of the time."

"She's nice to *you* because you're sweet on her, Gregory!"

Mr. McGuire turned red in the face and sputtered. "Well, that's just silly!"

Franny winked at me. "Anyway, when I mentioned turning the guy in, he told me he would fix it so I wouldn't be able to sell my animals, let alone walk in the streets in broad daylight. His exact words, if you can believe it, were, 'You shall rue the day you tangled with me!'

"I mean, who talks like that? But a week or so later, the guy calls me back. He asks if I've changed my mind. I just laughed again, and he says, 'A pox upon you and your enchanted menagerie,' and then this jolt of magic comes zinging out of the phone, and it felt like my head was on fire!

"Next thing I know, I'm sporting the first of these oh-so-charming boils, and my animals came down with all sorts of strange ailments," Franny said. "It's gotten worse every day, and you can see how the hex has progressed over the month. He must have transmitted the spell through the phone line. A sophisticated and very nasty trick."

"Those were Franny's frogs I was de-warting when Milo interrupted yesterday," Mr. McGuire said.

I gulped at the sound of Milo's name. I wanted to tell Mr. McGuire about his visit, but I didn't want him to know I had given Raphael the magic book to keep him from coming down to the shop.

"Hey," I said, suddenly making a connection. "Don't you think it's weird that some guy wanted to sell Franny rabbits and then Milo comes in with his bunch? Do you think Milo could've hexed her?"

"Doubtful," Mr. McGuire said, shaking his head. "A magician of Milo's caliber performs an incredible amount of shows—shows he is paid quite handsomely for. I can't imagine he'd have the time or desire to bother with rabbits, and Franny was hit by her spell over a month ago. No more than a coincidence, I'd say."

I shrugged. "Yeah, I guess he doesn't seem like the kind of guy who would be into raising bunnies, but when Franny asked 'Who talks like that?' Milo was the first person I thought of."

"Milo *does* have a rather unusual way of speaking," Mr. McGuire said. "And a lot of odd things have happened since he arrived back in town. Tell you what—I'll put in a call to Viola and see if she has any information on him. Which reminds me." He pulled a piece of paper out from a manila envelope, took several thumbtacks out of a jar, and stood up on a stool to hang a poster on the wall behind the counter. "This arrived from Viola today."

"Not another one," Franny said quietly.

"Roland the Rainbow Magician hasn't been seen or heard from in over a week," he said.

"Is he from around here?" I asked, looking at the picture of an old man wearing a rainbow-striped jester's hat.

"Yes, he disappeared on his way to the Downtown Cabaret Theater only about five minutes from here. All of the missing magicians have been local."

"I hate to interrupt you, Holmes and Watson, but what about me?" Franny asked. "I'm the one with the face only a zombie could love, and I have a dinner date tonight. He's an open-minded sort of fellow, but staring across the table at this would definitely kill his appetite. I say fix the face now, play detective later."

"You're right, Franny," Mr. McGuire said. "Let's hit the books! I'll be in the back room reading." Mr. McGuire removed a small, lumpy oval from his pocket and handed it to Franny. "I've got a pot of egg shaper ready to boil. Once it's ready, I'll mix it in your dove's feed. Hopefully this will be the last misshapen egg."

Franny smiled. "The rabbits are responding well to those pellets you gave me; they're starting to regrow their fur."

"Good, and I believe the frogs' warts are under control," Mr. McGuire added. "The syrup I've been applying seems to have done the trick."

"Can't we just put the syrup on Franny, too?" I asked. "Or maybe I could try to wish the sores away?" I asked hopefully.

"I'm afraid not," Mr. McGuire said, shaking his head. "That syrup is strictly for amphibians, and, unfortunately, hexes like this are too powerful for even the strongest wish magic. Since I've never encountered this particular spell, we'll have to hit the books and do some research. I'm sorry—your magic lessons will have to wait awhile, Maggie."

"That's okay," I said. "I've helped my folks do research in the university's library tons of times—only this will be a lot more interesting than the reproductive cycle of dung beetles."

Mr. McGuire raised a fist in the air. "That's the spirit! Why don't you start with the *Harry Hausen's Hex* reference set on the shelves? It's right under that jar of banana slugs. Look up poxes, wire transmissions, revenge spells, and anything else you can think of. If nothing turns up there, you can help Franny look through some of these obscure spell books I dug out of storage. I'll do some reading in the back room, where I can keep an eye on the egg brew."

After an hour of sitting on the floor, sifting through books detailing the most horrible hexes a person could suffer, I stood up and hobbled stiffly over to the counter, where Franny was hidden behind her own stack of books. "Find anything?" I asked, stretching my legs out behind me.

"Not unless you want to break the spell that's dried up your cows' milk, or keep fairies out of your larder. These books are ancient. I wouldn't be surprised if they were older than Gregory," she said loudly.

"I heard that," Mr. McGuire called out from the back room. He came through the curtains, smiling. "Taking a break?"

"I guess," Franny said softly. She shut the large book she was reading, sending up a tiny cloud of dust, and coughed. "I'm sorry my problem is eating up so much of your time."

"I still don't get why someone would waste their time casting a spell like this, anyway," I said. "Why don't people use magic to, like, feed the hungry or stop wars?"

"That's a nice idea, Maggie," Mr. McGuire said. "But it's not wise to fool around with the way things were meant to be. Not to say some magicians don't try, but everyone has his or her own idea about how the world should work. Who's to say what's right?"

"But what's the use in having magic, then?" I asked. "What good is it?"

"Magic isn't a choice," Franny said. "It's something a few of us are born with. The hard part is figuring out what to do once you realize you've got it." Franny leaned forward, looking serious. "Magic can either open you up to the most wonderful things imaginable, or it can corrupt your soul. A lot of people, like your grandfather, find it better to simply forget it was ever a part of them. Too many things can go wrong."

"Is that what he did, just walk away from it all?"

Mr. McGuire looked down at the ground.

"That would explain why my dad never said anything." My temples started to throb. I closed my eyes and massaged the sides of my forehead with my fingertips. When I had met Mr. McGuire, I had thought I'd slip into this wonderful magical world and my life would be perfect. I hadn't thought there could be a downside.

My stomach rolled into a nervous knot when I thought about how great it felt to have power over Raphael, and how easy it was to make him do what I wanted. And my parents—I mean, I was pretty sure I'd wiped out their memory of an *entire* day just so I could work in the shop. It wasn't hard to imagine how a person could get carried away.

I'd be more careful, I promised myself.

"Don't worry, Maggie," Mr. McGuire said. "The more you learn about magic, the more you'll understand."

"Well, all I can say is, whoever did this to Franny doesn't know who he is dealing with."

11

Magical Makeover

"I found it!" I shouted.

Mr. McGuire and Franny raced over to the book opened in front of me. "It's in *Diabla's Big Book of Disfigurement Spells*. Right here," I said, pounding the page with my finger, "it tells how to cast the one Franny got, *and* how to break it."

Franny gave me a high five. "Now my date won't lose his appetite when he gazes adoringly at me across the table tonight!"

"What's bladderwort?" I asked. "We need it to break the spell."

"It's an aquatic plant with floating bladders—I have

a jar on the shelf," Mr. McGuire said as he placed his glasses on his nose to get a better look at the book.

I pointed to a list of ingredients. "We also need 'the blood of ten blister beetles,' 'ground-up crustacean exoskeletons—preferably barnacles,' and 'a teaspoon of pollen from a corpse flower.'"

"It may all seem strange," Mr. McGuire said, reading my expression. "But it makes some sense when you look at the spell we need to repair. Franny has blistering, wart-like pustules covering her face—"

"Thanks for the vivid description," Franny said.

"Anyway," Mr. McGuire continued, "bladderwort and blister beetles each have a word that sounds something like her problem. Sometimes the name of the ingredient is more important than the ingredient itself, but I should have thought of the corpse plant—the flower smells like a decaying animal. That odor will definitely help break this spell!"

"Do you even have all of this stuff?" I asked.

"Everything but the blister beetles," Mr. McGuire said, "but I can conjure them up with a spell. I just need to come up with a rhyme." He got some paper and a pencil and began to write. "Hmmm. What rhymes with *beetle*?" he asked.

"Tweedle," Franny said, giggling.

"Never mind, I'll figure it out myself." Mr. McGuire erased a bit and wrote some more. He nibbled on the pencil tip, then looked up. "It's silly, but it should work. Maggie, get an empty jar, please. There are some in the back."

I found a small, wide-mouth jar and brought it out. "Hold the jar in your hand, Maggie. I think you'll like this." He picked up his crooked wand from the counter and held it over the jar. *"Blisters on faces, but not on the knees . . . ,"* he started in a deep, serious voice.

I grinned at Franny, who snorted, trying to contain her laughter. Mr. McGuire glowered at us. "Just keep that jar steady." He waited until we were under control and began again. *"Blisters on faces, but not on the knees, Franny's in trouble, and we all plead; bring us the beetles that Franny needs."*

I gave a start as ten brown beetles appeared in the jar, crawling frantically in circles. "Whoa!"

"Yes, sir," Franny said. "I've been in the magic business for thirty some years, and this stuff still amazes me."

"But how come you couldn't just *wish* they would appear?" I asked, peering into the jar, listening to the clatter the beetles made as they crawled over one another.

"Your wishes are actually a very basic form of conjuring—basic and sometimes inexact. Have you ever wished for something and it didn't come out quite like you imagined?"

"Yeah. I wished for butterflies but got moth *caterpillars* instead—and when I wished Milo's rabbit would appear, it didn't."

Mr. McGuire nodded. "In that particular case your wish didn't work because there are spells to keep rabbits happy and hidden in the hats until someone disarms the magic by tapping the brim. But you used your magician's intuition to figure out where the real rabbit was. Intuition is the perfect complement to talent.

"The more complicated magic spells depend on rhymes, puns, or similar-sounding words to make them work properly. No one is really sure why, but if you've got the ability, a silly rhyme or play on words can produce miracles."

He took the jar, inspected the beetles, and then turned back to me. "Now, I believe the bladderwort is over there with the herbs. What else do we need?"

"Okay, Maggie, we've got just about everything. Are you ready to handle the spell?" Mr. McGuire asked.

My heart beat a little faster. *"Me?"*

"No worries, kiddo," Franny said. "It's only my face."

Franny winked, but all the same, my stomach turned

nervously. The last thing I wanted to do was make her face look worse than it already did.

Mr. McGuire shook his head. "Just follow the directions—there won't be a problem."

"If you say so." I looked at the book and got to work.

I spooned out some bladderwort, crushing the green leaves with a mortar and pestle. Scraping the mash carefully into a small beaker filled with greenish beetle blood and ground barnacles, I imagined I was a mad scientist concocting a vile potion. I glanced back in the book, and frowned.

"Um, this is kind of gross." I looked up at Franny, my face turning red. "Sorry. I didn't mean it to sound that way. But I need some, uh, *pus* stuff from your skin."

"Charming," Franny said, scrunching up her nose. "Ah, well. Spread the wealth; take as much as you want."

Mr. McGuire handed me a medicine dropper. "Thanks. I think." Grimacing, I sucked up two milliliters of the disgusting goo and squirted the thick yellow liquid into the beaker. "Almost done," I said, looking at the spell book. "We need a dash of origins powder. That's the stuff you used on the rabbits, right?"

"Yes, the powder helps get things back to their original state," Mr. McGuire said.

I pinched a bit of powder into the beaker, then opened

the jar with the corpse flower pollen. "Oh!" I coughed and plugged my nose. "Dat's disgusting!" I dipped a teaspoon into the jar, then dumped the pollen into the beaker and quickly screwed the top back on.

I placed the mixture on a small burner Mr. McGuire had lit and stirred it with a spoon. A thick, swampy odor began to fill the shop as the concoction turned into a gooey, black paste.

I coughed again and turned the burner off. "I think it's ready."

Mr. McGuire picked up the beaker with an oven mitt and started to blow on it, then placed it on the counter. He took a wand, stirred it a bit more, and then handed it back to me.

"Okay, now I have to cover your face with this," I told Franny.

"Go easy on me, Maggie," Franny said. "I have delicate skin."

Mr. McGuire handed me a small sponge, and I dipped it into the beaker and dabbed the smelly gunk on her skin. "Don't take this the wrong way, but I hope my next magic repair job involves something a little less—"

"Revolting?" Franny asked.

I nodded.

"Me too," Franny said.

"Now what?" I asked, covering up the last bit of Franny's chin.

Mr. McGuire smiled at me. "Now you come up with a spell."

"*I* do?"

"You made up the mixture, you make up the spell," Franny said. "Any silly thing will do."

I chewed my lip, thinking. "Is there some trick to casting spells? Do I need to concentrate on Franny or the sores or anything?"

"Look at Franny and just say it, Maggie, but"—Mr. McGuire took a box out from behind the counter—"this will help focus the spell."

I opened the box and saw a shiny, black wand, curled and bent like a branch of an old gnarled tree.

"It was your grandfather's. He had it custom-made, and I know he'd want you to have it."

I picked up the wand and felt it vibrate softly in my hand. Sparks flitted out of the tip as I held it.

I bit my lip and took a deep breath. "I think I'm ready." I closed my eyes and winced, realizing I was gripping the wand so tightly, my fingernails were digging into my palm. I was suddenly worried—worried that wishing for stuff was all I could do.

I opened my eyes and looked at Mr. McGuire and

Franny staring at me. "Go on, Maggie," Mr. McGuire said.

Franny nodded. "Yeah, hurry, I feel like my face is cracking off."

I took a deep breath and waved the wand at Franny. *"Bubble, bubble, boils and trouble, remove this hex on the double!"*

I waved the wand around Franny's face and then stared at her, looking for signs of improvement. "I don't think it worked. Did it?"

"Only one way to find out," Mr. McGuire said. "Wash it off, Franny."

Franny bent over the sink, and I looked at Mr. McGuire, amazed to see he looked so calm when I felt so frantic. "Well?"

Franny stood with her back to us, patting her face with a towel. I could see her reach up and touch her cheek.

"Yee haw!" Franny said, turning around, her face free of blemishes. "I'm gorgeous again!"

My heart danced. "I did it! I'm a magic repairperson!" I twirled in a circle. "I can't believe I did it." I stopped dancing and stared at Franny. Without the boils on her face, Franny did look gorgeous. Her skin was smooth and milky, and with her halo of red curls, she looked like an angel.

Franny patted her cheeks. "That was by far *the* best

magic trick I've ever seen! I may need a copy of that spell, because I think you even got rid of a few wrinkles, too. So, what do I owe you, Gregory?"

"It's on the house, Franny. If you wouldn't mind, though, I would appreciate your opinion on this yellow cat I've been keeping. Its owner, Dagmar Olgaby, came in a month ago. She's been in the shop before, buys herbs and things, mostly for housecleaning magic. She's a full-time maid, part-time witch. She uses spells to make the cleaning go faster. Anyway, until the night before she came in, she claims the cat was jet black."

"I wondered about that cat," I said. I looked around the shop until I spotted it high on a shelf. "His fur is so bright, it almost glows."

"Did she say what happened just before it turned yellow?" Franny asked, looking at the cat with narrowed eyes.

"That's the strange part. Dagmar had just taken a new position as a live-in housekeeper for some gentleman. After cleaning all day, she said she sat down in an easy chair to rest. The last thing she remembers is the cat jumping into her lap before falling asleep. When Dagmar woke up, she felt a little queasy and was amazed to see it was midnight. The cat was still in her lap—only it was bright yellow."

"Was anyone else in the room?" Franny asked. "Was the owner home?"

"She said the owner wasn't due back until the next day. The other strange thing is that I haven't heard from her since she dropped the cat off. She said she would call to check in, but never did. I've been so busy; I haven't tried to get in touch with her. I'm not even sure where I put her new phone number. Luckily, it's a nice cat and it seems content staying here in the store. He's earning his keep too! There haven't been nearly so many mice around."

Mr. McGuire paled a little and turned to me. "I wouldn't mention that to your friend Raphael. He seems to have a fondness for the little guys."

I nodded.

"Let me take a closer look at him," Franny said. She dragged a stool over to the shelf the cat was sleeping on and climbed up. She pursed her lips, made kissing noises, and then lifted him down. The cat gave a sleepy meow and purred in Franny's arms as she stroked its lemon yellow fur.

"Oh, yeah!" she said. "He's definitely been hit with some kind of spell. He's practically vibrating with magic. I'm not sure what got him, though. That's your department, Gregory. But there's no doubt he's been magically altered. He's a real sweetie pie, though," she cooed, scratching the cat under his chin. "What's his name?"

"Otto, and I think he'll have to be content with his yellow fur for a bit longer. Right now he's at the bottom of my list of things to do. And while we're on the subject, here's twenty dollars, Maggie. I thought, as my new assistant, you could go to the market across the street from your apartment and get Otto some more food and a bag of kitty litter. When you get back, his box needs changing."

"Seriously?" I asked.

Mr. McGuire raised an eyebrow.

I wrinkled my nose. "Yeah, okay."

"Before you go, I want to thank you for your help," Franny said, walking over to me. She held out her hand, and as I shook it, she slipped something into my palm. "Shh," she whispered. "You earned it."

I opened my hand and saw a fifty-dollar bill. "But—"

"You better get that cat litter," Franny said loudly as she pushed me toward the door. "The litter box is smelling worse than a corpse flower!"

I stuffed the money into my pocket as the door shut behind me. I'd just gotten *paid* for my first job!

When Gram got home that afternoon, I was ready for her questions. I'd already decided I wasn't going to tell her much of anything. I didn't think she'd be too thrilled if she knew I was put in charge of de-hexing Franny.

"I'm sorry I'm late," she said. "How did things go today?"

"It was fine," I said with a shrug. "The shop needed a lot of cleaning, and I looked at some books. Oh, there were some neat pictures of Grandpa. In one he has a big snake wrapped around his neck."

Gram's eyes got hard.

"And, uh, I got to do some cool things and . . ."

"And what?"

"And I guess it was kind of fun."

"That's it? *It was kind of fun?* I'd like a few more details than that." Gram put her hands on her hips. "Well?"

"Well, I helped Mr. McGuire find a, uh, a recipe for this lady who raises animals."

"And?"

"And I had to clean out a litter box."

Gram put some lettuce in a colander in the sink. "So nothing out of the ordinary happened today, then? *You* didn't do anything special?"

"Nope, mostly I, uh, helped get rid of some gross stuff that was oozing around."

Gram seemed to relax a bit. She even kind of smiled at me.

"Well, how about a hand with dinner? I thought I'd make a fancy meal to celebrate your first day of school tomorrow. How does spaghetti and meatballs sound?"

I knew Mom must've told her that was my favorite meal, and I couldn't help feeling that Gram was finally making an effort to be a little more grandmotherly. "Sounds great. I'll make the salad."

Gram handed me a cucumber. "So what *fun* things does Gregory have planned for your next visit?"

"Just some more cleaning." I wrinkled my nose so she'd think I wasn't looking forward to it, but as I started to fill the pot with water, I couldn't help but get excited about cleaning a real live witch's cauldron this weekend.

12

Vote for Darcy!

"Well, what do you think?" I asked Hasenpfeffer as I twirled around in my school uniform.

He sat up and squinted at my legs. "Have your knees always been that knobby?"

"What?" I bent down and frowned. "Knobby?"

"And you need to accessorize or something. The white shirt just washes you out. Maybe you could sew on some sequins or tie on a sparkly scarf. A little makeup wouldn't hurt either."

I tugged my skirt down a bit, wishing it covered my knees. "I'm going to school, not walking the red carpet."

Hasenpfeffer snorted. "Listen, I've learned a thing or two from being in the biz all these years, and drab and boring ain't gonna get you noticed."

"Who says I want to get noticed?"

"If you say so, but you just let me know when you want to liven things up—I could make you look like a star." He looked me up and down. "Or better, anyway."

I picked my backpack off the floor and flung it over my shoulder. "I'll keep that in mind. Hey, Gram thought I should join this club at school that does stuff like animal care and things. I could use you as my project and maybe get you out of the house sometimes."

"*Anything* that'll get me out of this room. I used to be a world traveler, you know."

"So you keep reminding me, but I'll try to get some information today. I'm sure Darcy Davenport will know—she seems to know everything," I said, rolling my eyes.

"Davenport? Where have I heard that name before?"

"Somewhere in your world travels, no doubt. I'd better get going—I don't want to miss my bus on the first day of school."

He let out a long sigh. "Have fun. I'll just sit here all day—alone."

"I'll get you a carrot before I go."

"Oh my, a whole carrot! That'll no doubt liven things up for a whole minute."

"Fine," I said as I headed to the kitchen. "I'll get two."

"And some parsley," he called out. "Did you get the parsley like I asked? You know I adore parsley. But don't forget to rinse it really well—I hate when there's grit in the leaves."

The small school bus bounced as it hit another pothole. I hugged my backpack tighter.

"Are you okay?" Raphael asked. "You look a little pale."

I nodded, but my stomach was doing a crazy dance as I scrambled to figure out how I was going to trick a school full of brainiacs into thinking I was just as smart as they were. With only eight kids in my class, it wasn't like I could fly under the radar.

Raphael had gone over the list of students with me after dinner last night, and I was more convinced than ever that doing well at the Black Rock School for the Gifted and Talented was going to be a huge magical undertaking.

"So," I said, trying to remember everything Raphael had told me, "Serena Gupta is the one who played the harp at Carnegie Hall when she was six?"

Raphael unzipped his lunch box and pulled out some celery sticks. "No, she played the Metropolitan Opera House when she was six—she did Carnegie when she five."

I shook my head. "Great. I can't even play the kazoo. Was it Maximilian Litmann or Sal Perez who helped design a robotic arm for NASA?"

"Sal Perez did the arm; Max just got a couple of poetry books published."

I slumped in my seat. "And besides being an amazing harpist, Serena's won the national spelling bee two years in a row, Darcy is taking college-level math, Nahla is some sort of whiz with plants, and you design rodent experiments for fun. I'm doomed."

"Don't forget I won first place in a local bagpipe competition."

I rolled my eyes. "So everyone's got some amazing talent—except for me."

Raphael rolled his eyes back at me and scoffed. "Are you *kidding*? You can make moths appear out of thin air. That's a million times more impressive than winning a spelling bee!"

"But it's not like I can do that at school."

Raphael crunched on the celery. "Why not? Who's to say you have to hide your magic?"

"Do you know anyone who is openly performing magic?"

"Milo."

I sighed. "Anyone who isn't pretending it's all just an illusion?"

"Well, no, but—"

"And when the Salem witches practiced magic, they got burned at the stake!"

Raphael waved a stick in the air. "Actually, they mostly hung the Salem witches—burning was more a European thing—but they weren't really witches, just some poor women falsely accused of witchcraft."

"*Whatever*. My point is that without my magic, I'll be a nobody in a class full of geniuses."

"I think you're forgetting you scored a hundred percent on the admission test."

I bit my lip. "About that."

Raphael sat up straight and turned to me with his mouth in a perfect *O*.

I hung my head and nodded.

"And that girl Fiona in our class?"

"She'd taken the test, like, five times already and hadn't scored high enough to get in. I had to help her."

Raphael let out a long whistle.

"I know I shouldn't have done it, but Darcy made

such a big deal about how smart she was and how inferior I was, and Fiona's been trying to get in for so long and, and . . . what was I supposed to do?"

Raphael squinted his eyes and looked at me as if he was trying to get a glimpse inside my head. "I've got it," he finally said. "You'll have to magically invent a talent. If you're extraordinarily good at at least one thing, maybe no one will notice . . . you know."

I gave him a look. "No one will notice that I'm completely *average* at everything else?"

Raphael smiled. "Right. What've you always wanted to be good at?"

Thoughts flew through my head. Singing? The piano? Geography? The word "geography" made me think of a globe, which made me think of my parents halfway around the world. A hollow feeling replaced the butterflies in my belly. I'd been so wrapped up with the repair shop, I hadn't had much time to think about my parents. But I suddenly realized there'd be none of Mom's after-school hugs or Dad forcing me to recap my day at dinner every night. I would even miss their endless talk about insects.

"Bugs!" I said. "I want to be an expert in entomology."

Raphael raised his eyebrows. "You know, bugs are just one order of insects—like, there are butterflies, beetles, and dragonflies, and then there are *bugs*."

"I think I remember hearing that one time," I said, wishing I'd paid more attention to my parents.

"Well, if you're going to cast a spell, you'd better make sure you do it right."

"Fine. I *wish* I knew as much about *insects* as my parents do." A shiver ran through me, and suddenly all the things I'd heard my parents talk about made sense. I knew what an exoskeleton was and all of the characteristics of bugs. "Bugs belong to the order Hemiptera, which means 'half wing,' and they've got a proboscis used for sucking plant juices or blood. And did you know that a cockroach can live for seven days without its head?"

Raphael grimaced. "You definitely sound like you know what you're talking about, but if you want people to sit with you at lunch, I'd avoid the cockroach trivia; it's a definite conversation killer."

I swatted him on the shoulder. "This was your idea."

"I was thinking you might want to speak seven languages, or at the very least become an expert kazoo player."

I looked out the bus window. "My parents are entomologists. They sent me here so they could hunt insects in the Amazon."

I turned to see him staring at me as if he couldn't believe it were true. "That's why you moved here, so they could go *bug* hunting?"

I nodded as the bus pulled up to the front of the Black Rock School. I folded my arms across my chest. "Insects are very important. There are over nine hundred thousand different kinds in the world, making up for over eighty percent of all species. The earth would die within two months if they disappeared."

Raphael shook his head. "I don't know how popular you're going to be with the other *kids*, talking like that, but our teacher, Ms. Wiggins, will eat this stuff up."

Raphael led me down the hall to Room 13.

He'd told me that Ms. Wiggins had moved up with the class every year since kindergarten. "She's different from a lot of the teachers here—kind of out there and *very* emotional," Raphael whispered as we made our way down the hall. "When Nahla's plants got eaten that time, Ms. Wiggins was weepy for over a week. And just wait until Max stands up and reads one of his poems—she practically needs a sedative to get through the rest of the day."

I followed him into our room and saw a tall, wiry woman with wild black hair cascading down her back. She wore a flowing red dress and at least six long beaded necklaces. She caught my eye and gasped.

"Maggie," she said as she rushed over and placed a hand on each of my shoulders. "You poor, poor tortured soul." She stepped in closer and lowered her voice. "I read about what happened at your old school. And I know firsthand how cruel children can be when faced with a mind such as yours; no doubt they *pushed* you to your breaking point. But don't worry, you're safe here among your true peers, and I will personally see to it that your shining star *blossoms* to its fullest extent here at Black Rock."

"Uh, thanks," I said.

"Time for introductions. Everyone," she said, spinning in a circle with her arms outstretched, "gather on the rug while I fetch the talking stick from its resting spot. I'm sure it missed our lively discussions while we were away on our summer sojourns."

I turned and saw Darcy Davenport put her finger in her mouth and pretend to gag. A girl with shiny black hair giggled. "Come on, Serena," Darcy said, "the *talking* stick awaits."

"Sal and Max, please join us," Ms. Wiggins cooed.

Two boys with their noses in books looked up with disappointment on their faces. "Do we have to start already?" the chubby one with wavy hair asked.

"Yes, Max."

He looked longingly at his book and then shut it. "Come on, Sal," he said to the boy with big round glasses who was sitting at the table next to him.

Sal stuck a bookmark in the center of the page and then shut his book too. "That's the trouble with school. We can't do what we want anymore."

I scanned the titles of the books they were having such a hard time putting down. *Advanced Robotics for the Space Age* and *A Year in Haiku*, which it seemed Maximilian Litmann had written himself.

I spotted Fiona standing off to the side. She was twisting one of her braids around, looking a little unsure as to what to do. I waved, and a smile broke out on her face as she rushed over. "Hi, Maggie," she said. "We took the test together, remember?"

"That's not a test I could forget," I said as we headed to sit with Ms. Wiggins on a rug decorated with moons and stars.

She grinned even wider. "Me neither. I got fifteen alumni calls that evening, offering to sponsor me. My sisters were speechless! I'm getting a heck of a lot more respect at home now, that's for sure."

"Really? That's great."

"Except . . ." Her smile faltered a bit. "After getting a hundred, I thought I'd feel—you know—smarter. But I still don't understand half the stuff my sisters are talking about. And . . ."—she tilted her head toward Ms. Wiggins, who was sitting cross-legged on the rug, unwrapping a long painted stick from a purple satin cloth—"I have no idea what a 'sojourn' is."

"Me neither."

"A 'sojourn' is a trip," Darcy said as Serena snorted at her side. "And you're standing on our spots."

Serena put her hands on her hips and nodded.

"I didn't see your name on the rug," I said.

"Maggie, come sit with Nahla and me," Raphael called out.

A girl with chocolate skin and dark, intricate pixie braids patted the rug next to her.

"The view looks much better over there, don't you think, Fiona?" I said.

Fiona gave Darcy a nervous sideways glance. "Yeah," she said quietly. "Let's go."

As we sat down, Ms. Wiggins smiled serenely at all of us. "I want to start off by thanking the universe for allowing me to be with all of you talented young people again this year, and for granting your former classmate, Wendell Skinner, the opportunity to travel the world in search of passion for languages." She grasped the orange painted stick tightly in her hand and held it to her chest.

"Which is something I have been *dying* to do my whole life, but on my teacher's salary I've thus far been unable to fulfill that *particular* dream."

I shifted uncomfortably on the rug and saw Darcy and Serena exchange looks while their shoulders quivered in an attempt not to laugh.

Ms. Wiggins sighed and placed the stick in her lap. "But as always, I will find fulfillment leading you all on your quest for perfection and enlightenment." She gazed at us adoringly and then held the talking stick out and gave it to Fiona. "Ms. Fitzgerald, you now have the talking stick in your hand, which means you shall command all of our attention. Please introduce yourself to the class and tell us of your passions."

Fiona took the stick and ran her fingers down it nervously. "I, uh, I'm Fiona and I am happy to be here."

"Yes, dear, go on," Ms. Wiggins said.

Fiona shrugged her shoulders.

"Your passions, dear—what is your driving force in life?"

"Um, I'm not sure what you mean," Fiona said, and then she dropped the stick. It bounced on the rug, and Darcy and Serena sniggered.

Darcy picked the stick up and pointed it at Fiona. "She means what are you good at?"

"Nothing," Fiona whispered as she took the stick from Darcy.

"Nothing?" Sal muttered to Max.

Max pushed his glasses up on his nose and stared at Fiona like she was some strange creature in the zoo.

Raphael mouthed the words "uh-oh" to me.

"It's okay, Fiona, dear," Ms. Wiggins said, her eyes dewy with tears. "I know you've lived in the shadow of your sisters for many years, and that has no doubt hidden your true ambitions from even you." She raised her hands in the air and spread them apart. "But we shall throw back the curtains until your shining star *blossoms* for all to see."

I tried very hard not to roll my eyes as she repeated her "blossoming star" thing again. "Is she always like this?" I whispered to Nahla, thinking maybe Black Rock wasn't going to be so hard after all. Ms. Wiggins was nothing like the hard-nosed teacher I was expecting.

"Just wait," Nahla whispered back.

Ms. Wiggins leaned in toward Fiona. "And we *will* find your passion, because we have ridiculous standards and quotas to meet, and if you don't blossom, I don't get my bonus, and then I'll never get to Europe."

She grinned crazily at all of us and then held out her hand for the talking stick. "So, let's hear from Maggie now, shall we?"

After I dazzled Ms. Wiggins with my *passion* for insects and the need to protect the earth's biodiversity, a cause my parents were selflessly championing, the other kids introduced themselves.

As Ms. Wiggins teared up with each overachieving what-I-did-over-summer-vacation speech, Fiona seemed to shrink.

Once everyone had gone around the circle, Ms. Wiggins gave the talking stick back to Fiona. "Perhaps hearing everyone's adventures has inspired you to dig deep and find an area you'd like to challenge yourself in? You will need to fill out a goal form for your sponsor after our little powwow."

I held my breath as Fiona fumbled nervously with the stick. "I'm, uh, kind of interested in laws. You know, being someone who makes them. You know—a what-do-you-call-it—a lawmaker?"

Darcy and Serena tried to smother their snorts of laughter and looked close to exploding.

Ms. Wiggins cleared her throat. "*Girls*, it's Fiona's turn to speak." She turned to Fiona and beamed. "I think what you *meant* to say is, you're interested in the *legislative* branch of government and that perhaps politics is a passion of yours?"

Fiona nodded. "Yeah, I wanna pass laws that protect

animals and even that biodiversity stuff Maggie was talking about."

Ms. Wiggins clapped her hands. "This is fabulous! Your sponsor, Congresswoman Gilson, is a huge environmental and animal activist, and she will just eat this up. Italy, here I come."

Fiona sat up tall with a new twinkle in her eye. "And I was thinking of, uh, running for class president."

Serena and Darcy's mouths both fell open.

Before Darcy could say anything, I jumped up. "Wow, I *wish* you would all consider how *passionate* Fiona is about this and what a great president she'd make!"

Everyone but Darcy turned to Fiona with a dreamy look on his or her face.

Max shook his head up and down. "I could write some haikus for your campaign posters."

"I could draw some animals on them," Serena said.

Darcy's face flushed angrily. "You can't, Serena. You said you were going to help me with *my* posters."

"But she wants to save *baby animals!*" Serena protested.

"Maybe you can help both of us," Fiona said. "What're you running for, Darcy?"

Darcy put one hand on her hip and fingered the gold-and-ruby locket hanging around her neck. "*President!* I'm *always* president."

Ms. Wiggins shook a finger at all of us. "People, we're forgetting the talking stick." She held out her hand and Fiona gave it to her. "I think Fiona running for president is just what we need to showcase a true democratic process. After all, Darcy, you've run unopposed all these years. But now it's time to transition to our monthly goal statements for our sponsors, and then we'll have some fun decoding those DNA strands Nahla brought in at the end of last year."

She gave a little wave as if decoding DNA were the same as learning the ABCs. "Just an amusing little activity we started for fun," she said to Fiona and me as we stared dumbfounded at everyone's excited faces.

Well, everyone but Darcy's. She was too busy whispering furiously to Serena.

"Nahla's father is letting us help him with some molecular biology projects he's working on," Raphael said.

I sighed. "Sounds like fun?"

"Fiona," Ms. Wiggins said, "Mrs. Davenport will be in later with extracurricular activity and student government information. Be sure to get an application from her."

Fiona nodded and we headed to our seats.

As Ms. Wiggins sat with Sal to discuss his goals, I got busy writing about my quest to promote bio-diversity.

Suddenly a tightly folded note bounced off my arm. I picked it up and braced myself as I unfolded the paper.

I know something's going on,

and I'm going to find out what it is,

Bug Girl.

~D

13
The Kindness
of His Heart

Fiona raised her hand. "Ms. Wiggins, I think I found the answer! It's in the last sequence of amino acids."

Ms. Wiggins, Raphael, Sal, and Nahla rushed to Fiona's desk. Max and I, who sat on either side of Fiona, pulled our chairs across the aisles and watched as she pointed to her DNA strip. "Look, the amino acids on *this* strand are slightly different from the potatoes susceptible to blight. If Nahla's father can clone the potatoes with this DNA marker, it would mean an end to the disease."

"And more potato chips for everyone," Max declared.

Everyone's heads bobbed up and down as Fiona pointed out a subtle difference in the colored codes we'd been examining for the past half hour.

Ms. Wiggins threw a fist in the air and whooped. "You, Ms. Fitzgerald, are off to an impressive start!" She looked out the window, a dreamy look on her face. "I'm finally going to Europe. I can feel it in my bones."

"I can't believe I missed that," Sal moaned.

"How did my *dad* miss it?" Nahla added.

Max gasped and suddenly sat up straight in his chair. His eyes stared blankly ahead as he tapped his fingers in the air.

Raphael leaned down close to my ear. "He's composing a poem in his head," he whispered.

Max blinked and then recited his newest haiku. "Potatoes shall grow, black blighted tubers no more, Fiona we thank."

Ms. Wiggins clasped her hands under her chin. "Oh, Max," she said as her eyes watered up. "A fitting ode to the potato and our newest blossoming star."

Fiona beamed. "And to think I didn't even know what *amino acids* were until this morning!"

"Yeah, that's pretty strange."

I looked up and saw that Darcy and Serena had joined the group surrounding Fiona's desk.

"I mean, you didn't even know what *DNA* stood for," Darcy continued, "and then in under thirty minutes you go ahead and solve a problem that's baffled the top experts in the field."

Serena nodded. "Strange."

"Now, girls," Ms. Wiggins said, "I think *amazing* is more like it."

"Yeah," Raphael said. "You know I've read about people who have, uh, repressed learning."

"Repressed learning?" Darcy asked incredulously.

Raphael and I exchanged sideways glances. "Yes, I've heard of that too," I added. "It's more common than you might think."

"Huh," Fiona said. "Maybe that would explain why I suddenly knew how to do the calculus, too."

Darcy folded her arms across her chest and shook her head. "Repressed learning," she muttered to Serena.

Serena scoffed.

A timer went off, and Ms. Wiggins clapped her hands. "All right, children, why don't we take a breather and recharge our brains. I'll be at the rug meditating if anyone would care to join me. I have a new CD that combines the haunting call of humpback whales with the ancient chants of Irish monks."

Max sat up and froze except for his wiggling fingers.

"Oh, not another one," Darcy said.

She and Serena rolled their eyes and headed back to their seats as Ms. Wiggins looked excitedly at the rest of us, holding up two fingers.

"Two in one morning," she whispered. "At this rate he'll have another volume of poetry written by the end of the term."

After a few seconds Max blinked and stared up at Ms. Wiggins. "Mournful whales sing out, turning words into rainbows, on an isle of green."

Ms. Wiggins's eyes teared up, and her bottom lip quivered. For a second I thought she was going to have a complete breakdown.

"Oh, Max, that was *utterly* beautiful. *One of your best.* Come join me in meditation and perhaps the *rainbow* songs of the whales will encourage your muse to visit again." She led Max toward the rug, giving a dramatic performance of his newest haiku on the way.

"Hey, Maggie," Raphael said. "Would you give me a hand?"

"Okay," I said as he dragged me to the back of the room, where three bookcases had been set up to form a secluded alcove.

"Take it easy on the magic stuff," he hissed as a cacophony of whale calls and strange chanting filled the air. "You didn't have to turn Fiona into a PhD molecular biologist, you know."

I peered around the room to check that no one was lurking nearby. "I was just trying to help."

"And what about Darcy? I don't think she bought that *repressed learning* stuff."

I wrinkled my nose. "I know. I'll be more careful. I just wanted Fiona to fit in."

"Good heavens, it sounds like a cat is being tortured in here," said a woman's voice behind me.

Mrs. Davenport was standing in the doorway, searching the room for the source of the noise. She was wearing a purple flowered dress and had a pink clipboard stuffed with papers clutched in one hand.

She zeroed in on Ms. Wiggins sitting cross-legged on the rug and stormed over. "Alberta, turn that infernal racket off so I can speak to your class!"

Ms. Wiggins's eyes popped open, and she jumped up and turned the CD player off. "Oh, *Mrs. Davenport*," she said. "We, um, were just clearing our minds to prepare for an afternoon of grueling work—which will no doubt challenge your Darcy!"

"'Grueling' is how I'd describe being forced to listen to that caterwauling. But to each his own," Mrs. Davenport said, waving a hand dismissively in the air. "I'm confident you have some more educational activities planned for later . . . which Darcy will tell me *all* about after school."

"We've had quite a challenging morning, actually. Haven't we, children?" Ms. Wiggins said, her voice shaky and high-pitched. "Fiona here has made a scientific breakthrough that will change the agricultural world forever, and Max has already composed *two* new haikus."

Mrs. Davenport took a deep breath and forced a wide smile on her face. "Two, you say?"

Ms. Wiggins poked Max in the back. He stood up and recited his whale poem again.

Mrs. Davenport stared slack-jawed at him for a second and then pursed her lips. "That was . . . *lovely*, Max. It's a complete mystery to me why your poetry isn't selling better. I wish you could regale me some more, but I have other classes to visit. So let's get down to business, shall we?"

Ms. Wiggins clapped her hands. "To your seats, everyone. I believe the *talking stick* should go to Mrs. Davenport."

She held out the stick, and Mrs. Davenport's smile thinned. "Ah, the talking stick. Darcy speaks of it often."

Ms. Wiggins's brow furrowed, as if she couldn't decide whether this was a good thing or not.

"Children," Mrs. Davenport said, tapping the stick in

her palm. "It gives me great pleasure to welcome you to another year at the Black Rock School. As chairwoman of the extracurricular activities, I have all of the club information and forms you'll need."

Mrs. Davenport put the talking stick down on Ms. Wiggins's desk and then took some papers from her clipboard. "Student election forms, anyone?" she said, waving the papers about.

Fiona raised her hand.

"Yes, Ms. Fitzgerald?" Mrs. Davenport said, looking surprised.

"I'm running for president."

Serena nodded with a dreamy look on her face. "She wants to help animals."

Darcy glared at Serena as her hand shot up and waved in the air. "I'll take one too, Mother."

Mrs. Davenport gave her daughter a sheet, then walked to Fiona's desk. Fiona reached out for the paper, but Mrs. Davenport held it tight between two manicured fingers. "You're just *full* of surprises, aren't you?"

She let the form go, and Fiona's hand jerked back with the paper.

"I guess," Fiona said quietly.

Mrs. Davenport smiled and turned to the rest of us. "I also have information on the Mathletes, science fair, multicultural study group, and Country Values Club. Since you're so *interested* in animals, you should get a form for that, Ms. Fitzgerald. I'll come around and see who needs what while you all continue with your work."

When Mrs. Davenport had passed out all the papers, she walked to the front of the room again. "I have one more very exciting announcement. I want to invite you and your families to come to the school Saturday evening for a benefit performance of Bridgeport's finest magician, *Milo the Magnificent*."

There were snorts of laughter from several kids, but Mrs. Davenport focused on her daughter and cleared her throat. Darcy sat up straight and folded her hands neatly on her desk.

"Milo has agreed to do the benefit for our local food pantries out of the *kindness* of his heart," she continued, "so please come with as many nonperishable food items as your family can spare for what's sure to be a spectacular show."

I looked at Raphael. What were the chances Milo would be performing at *our* school?

Mrs. Davenport counted out eight sheets and placed them on Ms. Wiggins's desk. "I'm looking forward to seeing you all on Saturday."

When Mrs. Davenport left, Darcy sat up and stared

blankly at Serena. "I feel a haiku coming on," she said in a monotone voice.

Max frowned as he adjusted his glasses.

Darcy cleared her voice. "The lamest of all, a magician in purple, *stinking* on the stage."

Max muttered the haiku under his breath, counting the syllables with his fingers, while Serena laughed so hard, she almost fell off her chair.

"That's actually a pretty good one," Max said, giggling.

"Ha!" Sal laughed. "Remember Magic Manny from fourth grade?"

"He didn't even have a real rabbit," Serena said.

"And it was all so fake," Nahla added. "You could actually see the scarves balled up in his hands."

"The only good part," Darcy said, "was when he rode his unicycle off the stage."

"Children!" Ms. Wiggins clapped her hands. "I'm surprised at you. And I must add," she said, staring at Darcy, "that it was beyond cruel exposing all of his tricks—especially right after he had crashed into the orchestra pit. The poor man ended up with a concussion."

She put her hands on her hips and sniffed. "More important, let's not forget that Saturday's benefit is to help those in need, and Mrs. Davenport has assured the staff that Milo the Magnificent is a top-notch illusionist."

She stalked over to the rug and put her hand on the CD player. "I think it might do us all some good to join together on the rug and meditate on the fact that you all have promising futures that don't involve unicycles!"

She pushed the button, and Irish chants filled the air.

"It really was bad," Raphael whispered to me as we made our way to the rug. "He couldn't even juggle well."

"Well, we both know this show will be different."

The closing bell rang, and I blew out a puff of air. Fiona stood and smiled. "This was, like, the best day ever."

Darcy glowered at her as she hoisted her backpack over her shoulder and stalked out of the room, with Serena scurrying to catch up.

I buried my head in my hands. How could I keep this up for a whole year? I was utterly exhausted from making wishes so Fiona and I would appear to match our classmates' IQs—not to mention trying to sell everyone on Raphael's *repressed learning* hypothesis.

Then there were some magical mishaps to explain away.

When I had wished Fiona knew the chemical composition of glass, Max's eyeglasses had melted onto his desk. Luckily, he'd just taken them off to clean, and Raphael had cited a study in which eyeglass lenses were being made with substandard materials to cover the anomaly.

And when Ms. Wiggins had asked if anyone would like to translate a passage from the French book *The Little Prince*, my wish had backfired and I had stopped speaking English. I had had to excuse myself to the girls' room—in French—to make a counter-wish.

I couldn't wait until Saturday so I could relax in the shop away from the pressures of the Black Rock School, even if it would only be for a few hours.

14

Cauldron Burps

As I headed down the block Saturday morning, I heard Raphael call my name.

"Hey, Maggie!"

I turned and saw him running toward me. "I'm putting on a show this afternoon, and you *have* to come," he said, handing me a piece of paper.

I looked at it and saw he'd printed out a flyer that said THE AMAZING RAPHAEL—MAGICIAN EXTRAORDINAIRE. He'd drawn a top hat with his mouse, Pip, crawling out of it. "You're putting on a *magic* show?"

He nodded his head vigorously. "Yeah! I was reading

that book you gave me last night and decided to try some of the stuff, and something incredible happened. Wait until you see what I learned how to do."

"Do? Like magic tricks?"

He nodded again with a crazy grin on his face. "Yeah, *magic* tricks."

I waited for Raphael to wink or say "just kidding," but he just looked at me with wide, excited eyes.

I was totally confused. I'd thought only someone with magical powers could use what was in the book, and it was hard to believe that reading something *Milo* had written could unlock repressed magical power. A nervous feeling crept up my spine.

"So, like what kind of things did you learn how to do?" I asked, trying to sound very casual about the whole thing.

Raphael gave me a sly look. "You'll have to wait and see, but let's just say you are in for a *big* surprise. I've got some stuff I have to do before the show, but ask Mr. McGuire if he can come too. It starts at twelve o'clock. Don't be late!"

I walked through the door to the shop and immediately choked on something that smelled like a combination of Gram's smelly cheese and the squirrel that had died in our attic one summer.

"Ugh!" I said, holding my nose. "Do you have dat corpse flower duff oud again?"

Mr. McGuire hurried over and handed me a small jar of peppermint ointment. "Rub some of this under your nose—it'll help kill the stench."

I quickly dipped a finger into the jar and rubbed some of the stuff above my lip. I breathed in the minty smell as I dried my watery eyes on my sleeve. "That's better! Thanks."

"How were your first two days of school?"

"Not the best. My teacher is kind of crazy and so is half the class, but it was a million times better than this smell!"

I saw a cast-iron cauldron sitting on the floor by the sink. It was big, probably four feet across, and filled with a frothy, brownish liquid. "I take it that's what stinks?" I asked.

As if to answer my question, the cauldron began to bubble and churn, finally letting out a huge wet burp. Another blast of odor hit me as a cloud of buzzing flies magically appeared above the pot.

"Ew!" I cried, waving flies away from my face. "Can't you stop it?"

Mr. McGuire laughed again. "You'll get used to it. After a while you won't even notice the smell."

I looked at Mr. McGuire and saw he was wearing yellow rubber boots that came up past his knees, and a plastic flowered apron tied around his waist. "What do you have on?"

"This?" he said as he looked down at the apron. "This is my cauldron-cleaning uniform. I have a similar outfit for you."

"You're kidding, right?"

"You'll need to protect your clothes from getting mucked up. It's a dirty job, and," he said, clucking his tongue, "you're going into the pot."

"Into *that*?" I asked, gaping at the goo bubbling around inside the cauldron.

"This is what's called learning the business from the bottom up. We have to see what's making the cauldron burp, and lucky for me, you're just the right size to lean in and get a good look. Of course, we'll drain it first."

I smiled weakly at Mr. McGuire. "Of course. But how come the owner didn't drain it before he brought it over?"

"If a pot is drained, it has to be re-enchanted, which is a very lengthy process. A containment spell was cast on the cauldron to prevent the water from sloshing out during the move. Unfortunately, all of the preliminary tests were negative, so we'll have to empty it." Mr. McGuire held out a green plastic apron.

I took the apron and looked at the leprechaun grinning at me from the front of it. "'Kiss me, I'm Irish'?"

"You are Irish on your father's side, are you not?" Mr. McGuire said. He handed me a pair of rubber gloves and some oversize boots, and I followed him over to the cauldron.

"Be careful as you scoop the stuff out—the smell lingers if it gets on your skin."

"Great," I muttered as I started dumping out the most revolting stuff I'd ever seen or smelled into the sink.

So much for a relaxing day in the shop.

I stopped and looked up at Mr. McGuire. "Can I ask you a question?"

"Yes?"

"When we asked Gram if I could work here, why didn't you tell her I was a—you know—a magician?"

"Oh." Mr. McGuire put his bucket down. "I had planned on telling her, but for some reason I couldn't get it out."

"Because she was so upset about me coming down here?"

He nodded. "That's part of it, but I was more than a bit surprised you didn't know about your grandfather. I couldn't figure out why no one had told you. I racked my brain trying to sort the whole thing out. The funny thing is, the more I tried to remember the past—specifically the time after your grandfather quit—the foggier my memories became. I'm not as young as I used to be," he said, tapping his head, "but I feel like I should remember more. It's like looking through a dirty window; I just can't see the whole picture.

"At any rate, your grandmother seemed very upset about you coming down to the shop. I didn't want to spring the news about you just then. We *will* have to tell her, though."

"I guess." I picked up my bucket and slowly dipped it into the cauldron. "Is it possible someone could have magic powers and not know it?"

Mr. McGuire laughed. "Not likely. Magic is mostly inherited, but for those rare people who come from non-magical families, they find out the same way you did—wish magic. Seeing as children are always wishing for things they don't have, they make the discovery pretty early on. "

"So you don't think someone—I don't know—like *Raphael* could be a magician and not know it?" I held my breath, waiting for his answer.

He shook his head. "No. But funny you should use Raphael as an example. He visited me after school yesterday and asked the same question. I told him it was unlikely, but with him being as tenacious as he is, I finally had to give him a meter stone to hold to prove it to him once and for all."

"What happened?"

"Nothing. If he had any power—hidden or not—the stone would have reacted."

"Raphael is putting on a magic show at noon. He seemed pretty excited about it, so I was just wondering."

Mr. McGuire smiled. "I'm sure it's simple card tricks and such, but I think he might be trying to impress you."

"He asked you to come too."

"If I weren't so darn busy, I'd love to go. But let's get this finished up so you'll at least be on time."

I nodded, but with the way Raphael had acted when he had invited me to the show, I couldn't help wondering if Mr. McGuire was wrong.

When just a few inches of muck remained, I put the bucket down and looked at the brown slime clinging to my apron. "Thank goodness we're done!"

Mr. McGuire laughed. "Done? Why, we've only just gotten started. In you go, Maggie."

"I was hoping you were kidding about that."

"This will be a good way to familiarize yourself with cauldron repair—something I do a lot of."

"What am I looking for, anyway?"

Mr. McGuire handed me a flashlight. "You're looking for either cauldron shingles or ulcers toward the bottom of the pot. Shingles will be large pieces of flaking metal that overlap like the siding on a house. Ulcers will be in the form of pits or deep fissures in the iron. It's usually the older pots that get them. This one is less than a year old, but it has all of the symptoms."

I leaned over into the pot and felt a drip hit my arm and run down into the glove on my hand. "Wonderful."

"What's that? Find anything?" Mr. McGuire asked.

"Not yet." I turned on the flashlight and lit up the inside of the cauldron, revealing a crisscrossing of holes and tunnels. "Whoa!"

"What do you see?" he asked, looking in over my head.

"It's like Swiss cheese in here, except these holes don't go all the way through."

"So it is ulcers. Bruce and I were really hoping that wouldn't be the case. Hmmm," Mr. McGuire said, scratching his head.

"The witch's name is Bruce?" I asked as I stood up.

"Men can be witches too, though some people call them warlocks. Bruce uses his cauldron to turn quartz pendants into magic amplifiers. As a matter of fact, the pot went bad just after someone broke into his house and stole a bunch of his amplifiers."

"What does an amplifier do?" I asked.

"They can be used to temporarily increase a person's power. Many magicians use them to beef up their stage shows, or if someone needs to cast a spell that's just slightly beyond their ability. They're very expensive, so whoever stole the amplifiers either didn't have the money to pay for them or didn't want anyone to know they needed them.

"Bruce tried to use the cauldron to trace the thief— cauldrons can work like crystal balls—but the water fouled up, and it started burping flies. Fly burps can result from several cauldron malfunctions, but ulcers are the worst."

"So, how do we fix it? Do I hit the books again to find a spell?" I asked hopefully as I rinsed my gloves in the sink.

"No, this time it's a bit easier. We just need to caulk the cracks and holes. It shouldn't take more than an hour to get the job done." Mr. McGuire removed his gloves with a snap and began to untie his apron.

"Since you're taking that stuff off, I don't suppose you'll be doing the caulking, huh?"

"You won't have any trouble. The caulk is a little

sticky, but it's easy to apply with a Spackle knife. You need to be thorough, though. Cover the entire inside surface of the pot. While you do that, I'm going to work on a wand the Great Fabrizi sat on—something that happens more often than you might think. And I've still got to get in touch with Viola Klemp."

He leaned against the counter and pulled off one boot. "Anyway, the stuff you need is in a box labeled 'cauldron repair' in the back room. Make sure you get all of the water out and dry the inside surface before you start caulking. There are paper towels in the bathroom."

I looked at the brown globs that were dripping off my boots, making a jellylike puddle on the floor, and sighed. "When do I get to do something cool, like making duplicating rabbits disappear through a magic mirror?"

"When you work up to it. Now, get going—I'm sure you'll want to be finished and cleaned up so you'll make it to Raphael's show on time."

Mr. McGuire picked up the phone and started to push some buttons.

I nodded and looked at the clock on the wall, then back at the empty cauldron, shaking my head. I was actually looking forward to seeing Raphael's show.

An uneasy feeling crept up my spine. At least, I thought I was looking forward to it.

15

The Amazing Raphael

"For pity's sake, don't you know rabbits have a very keen sense of smell?" Hasenpfeffer said as I was getting dressed in my closet later. "Hiding in there doesn't keep your stench from assaulting my nose!"

I pulled my shirt over my head and opened the closet door. "I took three showers already! It just won't go away."

"Oh, I can't stand it," he moaned, hopping around in his cage. "It's like a combination of rotting meat and rancid milk!"

I sniffed my arms. "It's not *that* bad! Plug your nose if it bothers you that much."

"You know very well I can't plug my nose—I don't have opposable thumbs!"

"Fine, I'll see if Gram has any perfume or something. It's bad enough I had to caulk that disgusting pot, and now I'm getting grief from you. I can't believe I have to go to this show smelling like a skunk."

"You're going to a show?" Hasenpfeffer sat up, eyes twinkling. "Is it a musical? I simply *adore* musicals."

"It's not a musical! It's just this kid who lives in the building. I lent him this magic book Milo gave me, and he decided to put on some sort of show."

Hasenpfeffer twitched his nose. "*Milo* gave you a book?"

"Yeah," I said, running to Gram's room. I grabbed two bottles of perfume off her dresser. "What do you think," I called out, "Lavender Morning or Mystery of the Orient?" I sprayed each bottle into the air and sniffed. "Definitely lavender," I decided, sticking my tongue out at the other bottle.

I doused myself with lavender oil and sniffed up and down my arm. I still smelled a little funky, but it was an improvement.

I hurried back into my room and sat on the bed to put on my sandals.

"What kind of spells did the book have in it?"

"I don't know—I didn't read it."

Hasenpfeffer gasped. "You gave away a magic book without knowing what was in it? That's *highly* irresponsible."

"It's not a big deal," I said. "Mr. McGuire said the chances of Raphael being a magician were nonexistent, so it's not like anything is going to happen."

I left my room and snatched the key off the counter. I heard Hasenpfeffer rattle his cage, and then he came bounding down the hall.

"I don't think you should go," he said.

I shook my head. "How do you keep getting out?" I bent down and scooped him up.

"There's no need to manhandle me!" he squealed as I carried him back to my room. He squirmed and kicked as I opened the cage, forced him in, and shut the latch.

Hasenpfeffer jiggled the latch with his nose and nudged the door open again. "At the very least, I think you ought to bring me along to check it out."

"Would you stop opening the cage? Gram is going to put you in a stew if she knows you keep getting out!" I latched it again and took my wand out from the nightstand where I'd hidden it. *"Tick tock goes the clock, give this cage a rabbitproof lock!"* I folded my arms across my chest and smiled when I heard a faint click.

"There's nothing to worry about—so stay put, Houdini!"

"Fine! I'm just a rabbit—why would I know anything about magic?" he muttered, crawling under his blanket. He poked his head out and glared at me. "Oh, that's right—I've been starring in the magic biz since you were still wearing diapers! But you go ahead and feel free to ignore me and my expertise." Hasenpfeffer sniffed in my direction and sneezed. "Enjoy the show, Stinky," he said as he pulled his head back under the blanket. "I'm *dying* to hear how it goes."

When I walked down the apartment steps, I saw a small table covered with a checkered cloth on the sidewalk. A sign reading THE AMAZING RAPHAEL was taped to the side.

The Lubchek twins sat on two of the three mismatched chairs placed in front of the table. Anna Marie sang softly to herself, twirling her long black hair, while Anthony kicked his feet in the air and sucked on his thumb.

"Hi, Magnolia," Anthony said after taking his thumb out of his mouth.

"It's Maggie, remember?" I said.

Anthony nodded and popped his thumb back in.

"We saved you a seat," Anna Marie said, patting the empty chair between her and her brother.

I sat down and cringed as the old chair creaked under my weight.

"Isn't it neat?" Anthony said, pointing to Raphael's table before replacing his thumb.

"Yeah, real neat. Are we the only ones coming?"

"I think so," said Anna Marie. "There are only three seats."

Anthony took a few big sniffs, looked at me, and stuck out his tongue. "Ew! Did you fart?" he said, shuffling his chair away.

Anna Marie inhaled loudly and turned to her brother. "I'm telling Momma you said 'fart'! She sniffed in my direction and smiled. "And I think you smell pretty."

"She does not," Anthony said, "and you're a big tattletale!"

"When's this thing going to start?" I asked.

"Right now!" Raphael shouted, coming through the front door.

Raphael teetered down the steps, trying not to trip on an old yellow sheet he'd tied around his shoulders like a cape. When he reached the table, he took a cardboard tube covered with silver glitter out of a pocket in his overalls. Glitter fell like rain as he waved the wand in one hand and tipped an old brown derby he wore with the other.

"The Amazing Raphael has arrived!"

The twins clapped and cheered, and Raphael grinned as he put the hat and cardboard wand down on the table. He took out *Magic for Beginners* from another pocket, held it up and winked at me before he set it down on the table.

"For my first tr—," Raphael started until he saw Pip climb up from inside the hat and sit up on the rim. The twins giggled, and Raphael blushed and muttered under his breath. He tapped the rim three times with his wand, and Pip scurried back inside.

Raphael took a deep breath, narrowed his eyes, and looked each of us in the face. *"For my first trick,* I will summon the forces of magic and produce a bouquet of flowers for the very lovely Anna Marie."

Anna Marie squealed and clapped her chubby hands. Raphael twirled his wand around, chanting, *"Flowers, flowers, sweet to the nose, bring me some flowers, let them be rose!"* He reached under his cape and pulled out a gigantic bunch of yellow roses.

"For you," he said, giving the bouquet to Anna Marie, who giggled and kicked her feet as she wrapped her arms around the flowers.

I nodded my head and gave a little clap like the whole

thing was no big deal. But really, I was trying to figure out how he could've stashed so many roses under his cape without us noticing them.

I leaned over to get a closer look at the flowers, and the overpowering smell of fresh roses made me gasp. "Wait a minute," I sputtered. "Those are real! And they've been de-thorned. A bouquet like this must cost at least fifty bucks."

Anthony turned to me and rolled his eyes. "Who cares? Let him do the next trick!"

I glared at Anthony. "I just wanted to know how he did it, okay?"

"Silence!" Raphael bellowed. "A magician never reveals his secrets!" He smirked and raised his eyebrows. "Surprised?"

Surprised? I was stunned. I couldn't believe he'd really conjured up those roses, but I couldn't figure out how he'd done the trick either.

Raphael waved his wand in circles over the hat. *"Soar like the birds, buzz like the flies, I command this hat to start to rise!"* The hat began to levitate, slowly rising until it hovered two feet above the table. Raphael waved his wand above and below it to show there were no strings attached.

"Wow!" the twins said together, their eyes about to pop.

I stared at the hat wobbling in the air. There was no

way he could've faked that trick—the hat was magically levitating. "How did you . . . ?"

Anthony glared at me and I stopped midsentence.

"I told you it'd be cool!" Raphael said smugly.

Before I could say anything else, Raphael began to chant again. *"I may be little, I may be small, but this hat will drop, this hat will fall!"*

The hat crashed down onto the table, and the twins jumped up off their chairs, clapping madly.

"Again!" cried Anthony, who seemed to have forgotten his thumb.

"More flowers!" yelled Anna Marie.

"Raphael," I said, "something isn't right. You shouldn't be able to do this!"

"What are you talking about? *You* gave me the book!"

"But Mr. McGuire said you held a meter stone—he said you didn't have any powers."

Raphael's mouth dropped open. "He told you about that?"

"I was just asking if it were really possible someone could have powers and not know it."

Raphael narrowed his eyes again and walked around the table. He plucked a rose from Anna Marie's bouquet and held it up. "Well, it looks like it is possible!" he said as he threw it into my lap.

Anna Marie's bottom lip quivered. "Stop fighting!"

I looked down at her, and even though I had a really bad feeling about this, I smiled. "Sorry."

Anthony turned to me and stuck out his tongue again.

Raphael walked back behind the table, took a deep breath, and straightened his cape. "For my next trick, I will pull a mouse out of the hat!"

He tilted the hat toward us so we could see it was empty, and I knew it wasn't a trick. Pip was now magically hidden. Mr. McGuire must have been wrong about Raphael after all.

Raphael took the wand and began to wave it in circles above the hat again. *"Hibbity, jibbity, ribbity, zip; when I tap it three times, out comes Pip!"*

He tapped the hat three times on the rim and reached his hand into the opening. His arm sank up to his elbow, and then he pulled Pip out and held her up for a bow. The twins clapped as he put Pip back into the derby. He reached for the hat but jumped back as three shiny blue butterflies flew out and landed on the roses in Anna Marie's lap.

"Yay, butterflies!" Anna Marie cheered. "Again! Again!"

Raphael looked puzzled. "Um, I don't know . . ."

He reached out for the hat again and jumped a second time when several hummingbirds darted out and hovered over the table for a few seconds before zipping away. Then a loud caw echoed from inside the hat, and a crow hopped out onto the rim. The hat wobbled under its weight, and the crow jumped down to the table. It cocked its head, stared at us with glittering eyes, and then began to peck at the tablecloth. Raphael went to shoo it away, and the crow snapped at his fingers before it took off up over the apartment building.

"Raphael, what's going on?" I asked, getting out of my seat and slowly walking toward the table.

"I—I don't know—this stuff wasn't in the book," he said, wringing the cardboard wand in his hands, sending glitter down to the ground. "Pulling an animal out of a hat was supposed to be the last trick."

Anna Marie whimpered.

"What's the matter, Raphael? It's just birds and stuff," Anthony said. He looked back and forth between Raphael and me. "Right?"

"I, uh . . . look!" Raphael said, pointing to Milo's book.

Thin wisps of smoke were coming from the cover, leaving a rotten egg smell hanging in the air.

"I think the show's over," I said. "You two should go home."

A large wasp flew out of the hat and buzzed around

Anna Marie's roses. Howling, she threw the flowers down onto the sidewalk. As soon as the flowers hit the ground, they began to smolder and rot. More wasps flew out of the opening—and Anthony grabbed one of Anna Marie's flailing hands, and the two of them ran screaming into the building.

"Raphael, what's happening to the book?" I yelled, ducking down as several more wasps whizzed out and circled our heads.

"I don't know, it—"

The book burst into flames and within seconds was nothing more than a pile of ash sitting on the scorched tablecloth.

"Oh, this can't be good," I said, waving away some smoke.

The hat quivered, and Raphael and I exchanged worried looks. A huge bullfrog leapt out of the hat and landed on the table with a wet *splat*. Two more hopped out, and they puffed their throats and croaked in unison.

"You'd better let me handle this," I said. "I *wish* things would stop coming out." I shook my head. "There. That should be the end of—*Aack!*" I jumped away as another wasp buzzed out and flew right at me.

"I *wish* things would stop coming out of *the hat!*" I said more urgently. Another wasp flew out and landed on my shirtsleeve. I jerked my arm back and took three steps away from the hat. "Do something, Raphael!"

"I thought you were handling it!"

"Mr. McGuire said wish magic doesn't always work! Maybe you need to do it because it's *your* show."

"I don't know what to do—*none* of this was in the book!" Raphael looked helplessly at me.

"Forget the stupid book, make up a rhyme or something!"

"I can't think of anything. I—" Raphael cocked his head. "Maggie, listen."

Over the pounding of my heart, I heard a low humming noise coming from the hat. The sound got louder, and the frogs leapt off the table, shaking it as they went. The humming stopped, and I stared at the hat for a few seconds.

"What was that?" Raphael whispered.

I shrugged. "I don't know, but I think we should bring the hat to Mr. McGuire."

I took a few baby steps toward the table. I leaned in and craned my neck toward the hat, which I immediately discovered was a really bad idea. I jumped back as a huge swarm of wasps burst out and surrounded me in a noisy black cloud. I held my breath as tiny wings and legs fluttered against my skin.

I'm going to die, I thought, as wasps crawled over my eyelids and around my mouth and nose. I heard a strange sound over the droning in my ears and realized it was Raphael, whimpering beside me.

I needed to open my eyes. I needed to breathe. Cold sweat beaded up on my forehead, and I started to sway, thinking it would be a relief to just pass out. Suddenly I felt a stinger pierce through the skin on my leg. I screamed and flailed my arms, and the wasps flew up into the sky. I collapsed on the bottom step and looked up at Raphael standing like a statue, tears pouring down his face.

"It's okay, they're gone," I said quietly.

Raphael opened one eye and looked around. His shoulders slumped and he shuddered all over, rubbing his hands up and down his arms.

"Did you get stung?" I asked, shivering in the heat.

He shook his head and sat down next to me. "No, but I have never been so scared in my life," he said slowly.

"They got me," I said, pointing to a welt just above my knee. "I *wish* the pain would go away," I whispered. The throbbing stopped and I exhaled. "At least it worked this time."

"Do you think it's done?" Raphael asked, pointing toward the hat.

"I hope so."

He leaned over to pick up one of the frogs. "What should we do with these guys? They'll bake in this heat."

I wanted to tell Raphael that the frog was the least of our worries, but I had just looked back at the table and lost my voice as a giant snake glided out of the hat and coiled up on the sidewalk at our feet. I wanted to say all sorts of things like "run" or "help," but all I could get out was a hoarse kind of grunt.

"Maggie?"

"Snake," I finally managed, inching backward up a step.

"No, no, no, no," Raphael whispered. "This is bad. I think it's a cobra."

The snake—all six or seven feet of it—finished slithering out onto the sidewalk and reared up in front of us, spreading its hood.

Raphael whispered, "By the spectacled markings on its hood, I'd say it's an Indian cobra; they can grow to be . . ."

The snake turned its head and stared at Raphael with dark, unblinking eyes.

"Never mind," he squeaked as the cobra swayed back and forth, flicking its black tongue in and out.

The snake lowered its gaze, and out of the corner of my eye I saw the frog in Raphael's hand frantically kicking its legs.

"Drop the frog," I whispered.

"But—"

"Just do it!" I hissed through clenched teeth.

Raphael slowly opened his fingers. The frog hopped off his hand and landed on one of my sandals.

The cobra turned sharply toward my foot, its eyes locked on the frog. It lunged forward and snatched the frog before I had time to react. I inhaled sharply, and it took every bit of concentration I could muster to keep still.

"What do we do?" Raphael asked.

"I don't know!" Hot tears pooled in my eyes. "I *wish* the snake would disappear," I said quietly—knowing it wouldn't work.

The snake remained solidly in front of us and snatched another frog.

"If we stay still and don't pose a threat, it might go away," Raphael said.

"I'm not waiting to find out." I moved my arm slowly up to the handrail. In a flash the cobra turned to me and reared up once more. My breath came out in jagged gasps. Every inch of my skin turned to ice as the snake leaned in toward my face. Its featherlight tongue flicked the tip of my nose. I swallowed hard and shut my eyes, waiting to feel the sharp prick of fangs.

Suddenly a scream tore through my head. I opened my eyes to see that Raphael had grabbed the snake by the back of its head.

He kept yelling as they both tumbled to the sidewalk, knocking over the table. The snake twisted and thrashed until it finally broke free and rose up above Raphael.

"Maggie!"

I flew down the steps and grabbed one of the chairs. The cobra pulled back to attack, and I swung the chair, knocking it back midstrike.

The snake lay stunned for a few seconds, then twitched its tail. My chest heaved as I held the chair up, ready to hit it again, but it finally lurched away with a jerk. I dropped the chair to the sidewalk and plopped down on it as the cobra slithered into a storm drain.

Raphael groaned as he sat next to me, knees scratched and bleeding. He stared ahead at the hat lying on the sidewalk. "What if there's more? What if a Black Mamba comes out next? Their bite is fatal if antivenin isn't given immediately, and I have a feeling that's not something Bridgeport Hospital has in stock!"

We looked at each other wide-eyed, then turned toward the hat.

I ran my fingers through my hair and pushed my sweaty bangs aside. "It's been a few minutes since the snake came out—everything else came out one after another."

"That's true, and statistically, if something else were to come out, it already would have. You know what's weird, though?"

"*Besides* a venomous snake crawling out of a hat?" I asked.

"Yeah. Look around," Raphael said, waving a hand. "The street is empty—no cars, no people, no one who could've helped."

I looked up and down the block, surprised to see it unusually empty. "It's almost like someone cast a spell to go along with the nightmare magic show—someone named Milo the Magnificent."

Raphael turned to me. "This was all Milo—not me, right?"

I nodded. "He must've done something to the book."

He suddenly paled. "Pip! She's still in the hat. You don't think . . ."

I slowly walked over to the hat. "Mr. McGuire said there are spells to keep animals happy and hidden in the hats, so hopefully Pip wasn't sharing the same space as the cobra." I gently tapped the rim three times. Ready to run, I almost cried with relief when Pip crawled onto the brim.

"Pip!" Raphael scooped her up and kissed her on her pink nose. "You're not going anywhere near that bad hat again," Raphael said in a baby voice as he put Pip in the front pocket of his overalls.

"Let's get this mess cleaned up and head down to the repair shop to tell Mr. McGuire what happened." I picked up the rotten roses and dropped them into a trash can.

"Raphael Joseph Santos," screeched a voice from above.

"Uh-oh," Raphael said. "My mom."

I looked up at a woman who had the same brown curls as Raphael and was leaning out of a third-story window.

"What did you do to those twins? Mrs. Lubchek just called; she can't calm them down—she says they're hysterical."

"It was just a little magic show," Raphael said nervously.

"Well, you get in here and explain to me how a *little show* got those kids so freaked out!"

"I'll be right up!" Raphael turned to me. "I'll come to the repair shop as soon as I can—*if* I can."

"Okay. I'll deal with the hat."

"Be careful!"

Raphael sprinted up the steps, and I took a deep breath. I gently picked up the hat with my fingertips, held it out at arm's length, and started down the block. When I finally got to the shop, I looked down at the front window and noticed a small sign in the bottom corner: PROUD MEMBER OF THE SOCIETY FOR ETHICAL MAGICIANS—WITH MAGIC COMES RESPONSIBILITY.

I'm beginning to understand that, I thought as I reached the bottom. I opened the door and just about fainted when an ear-piercing roar bellowed up from the hat.

16

Through the Looking Glass

"Mr. McGuire, come quick!" I yelled, throwing the hat into the shop like a Frisbee. A low snarl came from the opening as the hat bumped to a stop up against the cauldron.

Mr. McGuire came out of the back room, carrying several folders stuffed with papers. "My goodness, Maggie, what's all the fuss about? Is Raphael's show over already?" He stared at the hat and gave me a puzzled look. "Why is there a hat on the floor?"

A roar came from the hat, and a large furry paw slowly reached out and batted the air a few times. Otto hissed from his perch on a shelf, leapt to the floor, and ran through the curtains to the back room.

"Lion?" Mr. McGuire asked, squinting at the hat.

"Yes! And if it's anything like the snake, it's on its way out and there isn't anything we can do to stop it!"

"Snake?"

"Milo gave me a spell book and I gave it to Raphael, and all this stuff started coming out of the hat and I couldn't make it stop."

Mr. McGuire's eyes widened. "A cursed book!"

Another loud snarl came from the hat, and Mr. McGuire bit his lip. "Cursed book, so we need . . . salt." He dropped the folders he was carrying on the counter and paced in front of the shelves. "Look over on the other wall. I know I've got a jar somewhere!"

The hair on my arms stood up as another roar pierced the air. I frantically scanned the shelves. My head began to pound, the labels blurring before my eyes. "I don't see it. It's not where it should be!"

A deep snarl echoed around the room, and I turned to see the lion's black nose poking out. It sniffed the air, twitched a few times, and then disappeared back into the hat.

"Oh, dear," Mr. McGuire said, hustling behind the counter. "We may not have time to find the salt. I think we need the mirror."

"The mirror? Why?"

Suddenly two large paws reached up and eight sharp claws sank into the rim of the hat.

"Because I'm deathly afraid of being eaten by a lion!" Mr. McGuire turned to the back room and ripped the curtains off their hooks as he struggled to get through them. "Quickly, Maggie!" he shouted, throwing the curtains to the floor.

I barely heard Mr. McGuire. The sight of a huge lion struggling to pull itself out of the tiny hat kept me frozen in place. The air filled with a musky odor as the lion shimmied and squirmed to be free. Finally out, the lion turned and gave the hat a long sniff. It swished its tail and growled, then picked up the hat and ripped it between its teeth and claws.

Mr. McGuire grabbed my arm and yanked me into the storage room. "Hurry, Maggie!" He dragged me toward the mirror and pulled the cover off. I gasped as the glass began to shimmer. A wet wind gusted out, blowing my hair back as it filled the room with the smell of rotting fish. The air whipped around and then seemed to get sucked back into the mirror.

"What's happening?" I cried as I felt myself being pulled toward the surface of the glass.

"The mirror is opening. Get ready. We're going in!" Mr. McGuire took my hand. "Jump!"

As he leapt through the mirror, I was jerked off my feet and dragged through the glass. A blinding light seared my eyes, and Mr. McGuire's hand was wrenched away. My arms and legs flailed, searching for solid ground as I turned helplessly in the foggy air.

Then I slammed feetfirst onto a wet, slippery surface. My legs buckled, and I tumbled across the moist, spongy ground. I caught my breath and sat up, wiping my wet hands on my shorts. I blinked away the echoes of light pulsing in my eyes, only to realize there was nothing to see. The thick, fishy-smelling fog danced around, leaving a film of chilly dew on my arms and legs. I shivered and pulled my arms around my chest.

"Mr. McGuire?" I called softly. I turned my head, listening. "Mr. McGuire?" I said a little louder.

"Right here, Maggie," he said, coming through the fog to me.

"Thank goodness!" I cried, standing up.

"This fog is thicker than I had expected." He looked around. "I wish I'd finished reading the instruction manual."

I stared at Mr. McGuire. "You didn't finish the manual?"

"Well, no." Mr. McGuire snapped his suspenders. "I was going to read it while flying to a conference I had planned to go to."

"Then why did you bring us in here?"

"Well, if the book you mentioned was indeed cursed, the lion could only be destroyed by salt, and I was afraid we wouldn't find it before the creature was completely out." Mr. McGuire looked down at his feet. "I also panicked a bit—I used to have dreadful nightmares about lions when I was a boy. Night after night I dreamed I was being hunted down by a pride of lions dressed in pink bikinis." Mr. McGuire blushed. "But don't worry, I've read enough of the manual to know we need to find the mirror's opening so I can alter the reflection."

"Alter it?"

"We need to get rid of the mist and create a reflection of the repair shop. And based on what I *did* read, we should be quick about it."

I turned in a circle, peering into the gray fog. "There's nothing out there," I said, picturing myself wandering lost in the mist forever. I sighed and rubbed my shirtsleeve across my eyes, too tired to know if it was tears or mist I was wiping away.

"There." Mr. McGuire pointed, his fingertips disappearing in the haze. "To the left."

I squinted at a dim glow ahead, feeling hopeful. "So why do we need to be 'quick about it'?" I asked just before something icy and wet slithered across the back of my neck. "Ahh!" I ducked down and wiped a hand across my neck and came away with a handful of thick, foamy slime. "Oh, gross!"

"That's why," Mr. McGuire said. He pointed to a large wet spot on his shirtsleeve. "I seem to recall reading about some sort of leechlike inhabitants, but I can't remember if they were dangerous or not."

"Oh, great! We're trapped in a magic mirror filled with fog and . . . and things that may or may not want to eat us."

I bit my lip as I looked around. "I thought this magic stuff would be so great," I said. "Coming down to the shop, meeting you, and finding out about Grandpa made me feel normal. I felt like I fit in somewhere. But this has all been . . ."

Mr. McGuire looked down. "I'm sorry, Maggie. I shouldn't have gotten you involved in all of this. I should have seen the danger signs." He sighed. "And I think you were right."

I sniffed. "About what?"

"Milo. When you came in, I was just starting to look through the files that Viola Klemp sent. She has quite a collection of paperwork on Milo, and I made a rather disturbing discovery. I found Dagmar Olgaby's new phone number this morning. It's the same number listed for Milo's Bridgeport home. Dagmar was Milo's maid—before her cat turned yellow and she disappeared, that is."

"I knew it!" I shouted furiously. "That creep's responsible for all of this. I never should've given Raphael that book!"

Mr. McGuire took off his glasses and rubbed his eyes. "Once a cursed book is opened, it releases a series of predetermined spells on an unsuspecting victim. The first few times they're used, everything goes off flawlessly, and the target is lulled into a false sense of security."

I sighed. "Raphael must've done the show once in his apartment. He was really excited—he thought he'd finally unlocked some hidden powers."

"It's usually the third or fourth attempt that sets off the 'joke' spells. Typically these books are used as pranks on novice magicians—I've witnessed ones that let off a series of small explosions or nasty smells. But snakes and lions are beyond the realm of a harmless prank."

I bit my lip. "I should've been more careful."

Mr. McGuire clucked his tongue. "What's done is done. But I don't understand why Milo would've given you that book in the first place. It doesn't make sense."

"I don't know, but as soon as we find a way out of here, he's going to get it!"

"As soon as we get out of here, you are going to your

grandmother's. I promised you wouldn't get into any trouble, and look where we are," he said, waving a hand at the fog. "I'm not going to put you in any more danger!"

I knew it was useless to argue, but I also knew I wouldn't be able to sit back while Mr. McGuire tackled Milo alone. Then I heard a pitiful meow and saw the bright yellow fur of Dagmar's cat running toward us through the mist.

"Otto! How did you get in here?" I asked as I scooped him up, feeling his heart pounding wildly. I ran my fingers down his back and grimaced. "Ugh, he's been slimed too." I put the cat down and pulled sticky clumps of fur off my hands.

"He must have gotten pulled in at the same time we did. If the mirror is uncovered without an instruction spell, it takes in any living creature within a three-foot radius before becoming inactive. The powder we used with the rabbits made sure only they would enter the mirror—and vanish. Fortunately for us, we can step out whenever we want to. But that wouldn't be advisable at this time."

"Well, I'm glad that lion wasn't close enough to get sucked in with us. We would've been pretty easy to sneak up on in this fog."

"Yes, the fog," he said, peering over his shoulder. "I

don't think it's wise to stay in one place too long. Let's keep moving." Mr. McGuire started walking toward the light. "I'd like to get rid of that lion quickly. It would be bad for business if it ate a customer."

When we reached the opening, I looked out into the shop. The lion was sitting on the counter, licking its chops with a long, pink tongue like there was nothing strange about its hanging around in a repair shop instead of the African plains. "You don't suppose he found something to eat, do you?"

Mr. McGuire peered out of the mirror and scanned the back room. "It looks like all of the cages are in one piece."

Otto meowed, and I bent down and smoothed his fur. "Good thing you came in with us. You would have made a tasty treat for that . . . Ack!" Something brushed against my head. I ran my fingers through a gooey patch of slime in my hair.

The odor of dead fish grew stronger, and then suddenly dozens of creatures were sliding against me. "Mr. McGuire, do something!" Sharp teeth nibbled on my shoulder. "Ow!" I yelled, knocking the thing to the ground.

I looked down and wrinkled my nose at the pale gray, eel-like creature wriggling around at my feet. It rolled over and I stepped back as it opened and closed its round mouth, showing off row upon row of pointy teeth. "Hurry!" I said as I kicked it away into a swirl of fog.

Mr. McGuire touched the inside surface of the mirror's glass with his palms. *"Mirror, mirror, make the fog stop; turn this world into the shop."*

Instantly the fog disappeared, and for a minute I panicked, thinking we were in the back room, inches away from the lion. "We're out?" I looked frantically around, and then I saw the mirror opening and understood. "We're still inside, aren't we?"

"The spell transformed the inside of the mirror into a facsimile of the shop, but because the lion was magically created, it wasn't copied. We need to find the salt on the shelves in here, and then we can rid ourselves of that beast out there."

I glanced out and watched the lion jump off the counter, scattering the files all over the floor. It padded over the torn curtain to the mirror. Mr. McGuire had said the lion couldn't get in, but I still took a step backward. "You're *sure* it can't get in?"

"Positive."

I inched back toward the mirror's opening and crouched down a bit so the lion and I were eye to eye. Grinning, I scraped a glob of slime off my arm. I slowly reached my hand toward the surface of the glass and flicked the goo through the mirror's opening onto the lion's nose. The lion snapped at my fingers, and I fell back.

"Maggie, stop teasing the lion and help me find the salt!"

"Sorry." I glanced back one more time, and my eye caught some movement out in the shop. "Oh, no!" I shouted. "Raphael! He doesn't know about the lion!"

"Mr. McGuire? Maggie?" Raphael called out as he closed the front door. "Guys? Where are you?"

17

Out of Thin Air

A chill went through my body as the lion turned away from the mirror and sniffed the air. Raphael looked around and called out again. "Maggie?"

"Raphael! Watch out!" I screamed.

The lion flicked its tail and in one powerful leap jumped back through the doorway and onto the counter. It raised its head up into the air and let out a tremendous roar. Raphael gasped and slumped to the floor with a thud as the lion leapt down toward him.

My heart skipped a beat. "Raphael!"

Mr. McGuire ran for the opening. "Find the salt," he

yelled as he jumped through the glass. "Just toss it out. Don't leave the mirror!"

I turned toward the shelves, heart racing. Otto meowed, and I looked up to see the cat sitting on a shelf, a large canister labeled DEAD SEA SALT directly beneath him.

"Thanks, Otto!" I grabbed the canister off the shelf and ran to the mirror's opening. Mr. McGuire was backing up through the doorway to the storage room, with the lion slowly coming around the counter, stalking him. The lion stopped and crouched, swishing its tail back and forth. Its shoulders began to twitch, and suddenly it sprung at Mr. McGuire, sending them both crashing into a pile of boxes opposite the mirror.

Despite what Mr. McGuire had said, I leapt through the glass and dumped the container of salt onto the lion, jumping back as the big cat howled and writhed, slashing at the air with its claws. Its fur began to smolder, and with one last roar it exploded into a cloud of sulfur, covering the back room with a fine yellow powder.

I raced over to Mr. McGuire and held out my hands to help him up. "Are you okay?"

Mr. McGuire groaned as I tugged him up. He looked down at his torn shirt and winced. "I've been better," he said, and brushed the yellow powder off his clothes. Bending slowly, he picked up his glasses and straightened out the frames. Placing them back on his nose, he smiled weakly. "I thought I told you to stay in the mirror."

"Good thing I didn't. You could've been killed!"

"I must admit I was getting a bit worried." Mr. McGuire picked up some rags and used them to dust off his shirt.

I looked through the doorway. "Raphael?" I asked, afraid to know the answer.

"Is it gone?" Raphael called out.

I ran around the counter, and Raphael was lying on the floor, arms splayed at his side. "Yeah, it's gone."

"Ow," he said, sitting up and rubbing the back of his head.

"Did you faint?" I asked.

"Yes, I fainted! Statistically speaking, it's rare to find a man-eating lion in a repair shop. When I saw one leaping toward me, my brain scrambled and I blacked out. And look at this disgusting mess," Raphael said, pointing to his wet shoes.

I wiped a patch of slime still sticking to my arm and flicked it at Raphael. "Try being *covered* in this mess!"

"Hey!" he complained, dodging the trail of goo.

"Really now!" Mr. McGuire said. "I'm surprised at you two. You'd think we'd just been menaced by a kitten instead of a lion!"

I dragged my teeth across my lip, suppressing a smile. "Sorry." I bent over and picked up the torn curtain, placing it in a heap on the counter.

"Well, we're all okay—that's the important part," Mr. McGuire said.

A loud meow startled me, and I turned to see Otto stick his head out of the mirror. The cat twitched his whiskers, then jumped through the glass.

"There's the real hero. Otto was sitting right above the salt." I bent down and scratched him under his chin.

"How did you know to pour the salt on the lion, by the way?" Mr. McGuire asked. "I never told you what I was going to do with it."

"I just knew, I guess. You know—intuition." I stood up and leaned into the pile of curtains on the counter, smelling years of dust in its folds. "I feel kind of bad, though. That salt really seemed to hurt it."

"I know, Maggie, but it wasn't real," Mr. McGuire said. "He looked and acted like a real lion, but he was made of pure magic."

"Magic with sharp teeth!" Raphael cried, poking his finger through a tooth hole in what was left of the hat's felt.

"Well, yes," Mr. McGuire agreed. "Magic can create things that can move, think, and, well, eat you. But it's not like it was a real lion transported out of Africa or even a duplicate of a living creature like Milo's rabbits were. It was created out of thin air." He took a pinch of yellow powder that had gathered in his shirt pocket and blew it away.

"He seemed real," I said, watching the powder float in a thin strip of sunlight peeking through the store window.

Mr. McGuire nodded. "In a way, he was. But you see, that's just the trouble. These creatures don't know they're not real. Maybe at the end, when the magic that created them is unraveling, they understand."

Mr. McGuire looked down at his chest and took a deep breath that ended in a painful cough. "Well, I'd better gather some things for a healing spell, and then we can get down to business. Raphael, where's the magic book Maggie gave you?" asked Mr. McGuire. "Did it disappear, or is it still in your apartment?"

"It went up in flames during my show."

"Ah, Milo was smart! He had the spell book self-destruct so it couldn't be traced back to him."

"I just want you to know that book didn't say anything about snakes or lions," Raphael said. "I never in a million years would've done that show if I knew what was coming. I just wanted to—you know—work down here with you. Like Maggie." Raphael blushed.

"You know you're always welcome down here, Raphael," Mr. McGuire said.

Raphael shrugged and looked sideways at me. "I wasn't so sure."

Mr. McGuire turned and glanced at me with raised eyebrows.

My cheeks flushed. "I know. I was a big jerk, and I'm really sorry."

Mr. McGuire nodded. "I just wish I knew what Milo was thinking when he gave you that book. It could very well be jealousy. Some magicians feel threatened by new talent. Milo seemed very impressed when you held that meter stone. Perhaps he isn't as powerful as he wanted us to believe."

I shook my head. "It's got to be something more. I mean, the guy sent a parade of killer animals after me."

"I can't think of anything unusual that happened the day Milo came to the shop—well, other than his rabbit trouble," Mr. McGuire said.

"Hey! Do you think it's weird that Milo's eyes were the same color as the rabbits'?" I asked. "And his chauffeur had gray eyes too. I've seen people with gray eyes before, but these were different—Reginald's are almost dead looking!"

"Uh," Raphael said, "unless there was some big scientific

study I missed, having gray eyes isn't a prerequisite for being an evil magician or getting a chauffeur's license."

Mr. McGuire nodded. "I have to agree—that sounds more like a coincidence than cause for incriminations."

"But Reginald's were *so* freaky," I said, bugging my eyes out for emphasis. "Maybe it had something to do with Otto." I looked over at Raphael. "Mr. McGuire just told me this lady, Dagmar, was working for Milo, until she dropped off the cat and disappeared. I wonder if Milo was afraid we'd figure out the connection!"

"Possibly, and maybe he assumed you'd use the book in the shop," Mr. McGuire said. "Of course, he would've been foolish to think I wouldn't recognize what the book really was. Maybe the information we need is in the files that Viola sent." Mr. McGuire glanced at the papers scattered about the floor and sighed. "You two go up to your apartment, Maggie, and I'll pick these up and meet you there."

"We're not going to leave you," I said, bending down and stuffing some papers into a file. "What if Milo comes back?"

"It's not safe for you two in the shop right now. I'm only letting you help because I'm running out of time, and if there's a mystery to solve, three heads are better than one. Milo's last show in town is tonight at your school. Who knows where he'll be tomorrow? If we want to stop Milo, we have to do it today. Head back to your apartment, and I'll finish getting these papers together."

"Okay."

I followed Raphael to the door but turned when a glint of light caught my eye. Following the slat of sunlight, I noticed a key shining on its hook on the wall behind the counter. Listening to the water running in the bathroom, I walked behind the counter, careful to avoid the warped squeaky board.

"He may not want my help, but he needs it," I said quietly to myself. I glanced back at the door.

"Come on, Maggie," Raphael called from outside.

"Coming!" I snatched the extra shop key off its hook and clutched it in my sweaty hand. A magician has to trust her intuition, I remembered.

18
Duplicates, Rings, and Rabbits

Mr. McGuire spread the files out on Gram's kitchen table. "What time did you say your grandmother would be back, Maggie?"

I looked up at the round clock hanging on the wall. "She said she'd be home by five o'clock."

"Let's get right to work, then," Mr. McGuire said. "Why don't we each take a folder and dig in. Maggie, you take this one. It contains newspaper articles about Milo and reviews of his shows. Raphael, you look through this one. It's filled with publicity material, flyers, and photographs—items that a member of his fan club might get."

"Who'd want to hang this face on their wall?" Raphael snickered, holding up a picture of Milo.

I laughed, seeing Milo dressed in a red velvet cape and hat, clutching his wand to his chest and leering at the camera. "You'd think he'd at least try to smile for a publicity photo," I added.

"Enough funny stuff, you two. Let's get going. I'll look through his personal information. Hopefully we can come up with something."

"What exactly are we looking for?" asked Raphael, rifling through some photos.

"Anything unusual. Anything that might hint at why he gave Maggie that book."

After half an hour I was squirming in my seat. The beginning thumps of a headache were nagging at my temples. "This is so lame! All of these articles and reviews just say how wonderful Milo is."

I held up a page and curled my lip in disgust. "And I quote, 'Milo the Magnificent continues to wow audiences across Europe. With his trademark velvet ensemble and dazzling special effects, his performances are a feast for the eyes and a chance to relive the magic of childhood. Milo is a modern-day Houdini.' Ugh! If I read another article telling me how fabulous he is, I'm going to scream!"

"He's not even that famous," Raphael said. "I didn't even know who he was until those commercials started airing on TV last month."

"Milo spends most of his time in Europe and Asia," Mr. McGuire said. "He's very popular overseas. He has a big house in town, though, and comes back to the States every few years to perform a couple of shows."

I picked up another article and scanned the headline. "Hey, I'd say this qualifies as unusual—listen. 'Master Magician Mystifies! Milo the Magnificent, known for his top-notch shows, perfected his illusion of mystery this week by performing first in Hong Kong and then minutes later popped up halfway around the world in Las Vegas, Nevada. When asked to explain how he was able to travel such a great distance so quickly, the magician simply told reporters, 'Magic.'

"'Unfortunately, traversing thousands of miles in a few short minutes took its toll on the star mage. At the Vegas show Milo was reported to have been less than magnificent. Reviewers agree that the Nevada show was sloppy and weak—the worst performance in the magician's illustrious career. Fans will have to hope Milo the Magnificent will have the old magic touch back for his next show in Amsterdam.'"

Raphael folded his arms across his chest and smiled smugly. "Milo has a twin. Case solved!"

"Not so fast. According to his records," Mr. McGuire said, "Milo was the only child of a very wealthy couple raised right here in Bridgeport."

Raphael's smile disappeared.

"Look, there's more," I said, laying two clippings out. "The show in Amsterdam got great reviews, but the one he did on the same day in Las Vegas got awful ones. And this one from the end of June says he's canceling his American tour for health reasons."

Raphael put both of his hands in his hair and gave a good scratch. "Okay. Let me see if I've got it. Milo started doing two shows a day—one in Europe, one in the U.S. The European show would be great, the other stinko. Right?"

"Right," I said. "Then he says he's going to cancel his shows in the United States, but he never does. He's toured New England all summer, but"—I shuffled through the remaining clippings—"I don't see any articles saying how those shows were, except this one talking about his successful re-creation of Houdini's water torture cell trick."

"Okay," said Raphael. "We know he doesn't have a twin, so he must be, like, magically sending himself across the world."

"Not likely," Mr. McGuire said. "Milo is powerful, but very few magicians have the power necessary to magically transport themselves from place to place." Mr. McGuire looked through his pile of papers until he came to a copy of Milo's magician's license. "Actually, he's listed here as a level nineteen magician. You'd need to be at least a level fifty to accomplish such a feat. Come to think of it, he would have to be a level thirty-eight magician to successfully complete the water trick." Mr. McGuire clucked his tongue. "So how did Milo get the extra power needed to copy Houdini?"

"What if he was the one who stole the magic amplifiers from the guy whose cauldron we patched up? Would that get him to level thirty, or even fifty?" I asked.

"Not quite. At the very most, an amplifier would increase your power by ten, maybe fifteen, levels for a short period of time." He clucked his tongue again and shook his head. "These things must be connected, but I can't put them together." He looked across the table. "Why don't we move on to you, Raphael? What have you got for us?"

Raphael spread several dozen photos and flyers on the table. "Well, when he's in the U.S., he lives on the other side of town in a really cool mansion right down the street from where one of P. T. Barnum's old places used to be.

He's also got really rotten taste in clothes. Check out these pictures," he said as he moved them around. "What's with all the velvet? Who wears this stuff? And"—he grabbed another pile of pictures—"as if the red velvet wasn't bad enough, he goes and switches to purple. He looks like a giant grape!"

"Wait, look!" My heart raced as I inspected some of the earlier photos. "Look at these. Look at his eyes."

Raphael scanned the picture and shrugged. "They're blue, so what?"

"So look at all of the purple velvet pictures. His eyes are gray in these."

"So he was wearing colored contacts."

"Or maybe they're not the same person. Maybe Milo duplicated himself." I turned to Mr. McGuire. "Could he do that? Could Milo make a copy of himself, like someone did with the rabbits?"

Mr. McGuire nodded. "It's possible. And Milo does have the power to carry off a tricky duplication spell like that. It's highly unethical, though. It's sort of an unwritten rule in magic. You're not supposed to duplicate things like rabbits, let alone people. The copies believe they're just as real as the original, and well, as you've experienced, things can get tricky."

"When I was looking for Milo's rabbit, you told me

it would be different from the duplicates. Milo used to wear red velvet. And now just when he comes back to the U.S., he starts wearing purple. His eyes were blue, and now they're a really weird gray just like the rabbits. He's got to be a duplicate."

"But if the Milo we met is a duplicate, how did he manage to get more powerful than the original?" Mr. McGuire asked. "For that matter, what happened to the real Milo?"

The three of us looked at one another, and I shivered at the possibilities.

Mr. McGuire stood up. "I think it's time to pay Milo a visit."

I nodded and jumped up. "Yeah. I have a few questions to ask that creep."

Mr. McGuire folded his arms across his chest. "You're not going, Maggie."

"But if he's so powerful, how are you going to protect yourself?" I asked. "That stone showed I have more power than you do. You need me!"

"I can't risk your getting hurt," Mr. McGuire said.

"But—"

"You're not going!"

"Fine." I sat back down and slumped in the chair.

Mr. McGuire smiled. "Cheer up. I have something for

you." He took a small leather pouch out of his pocket and dropped two rings into his palm. One ring was gold, the other silver. Each had an identical black opal in the setting. "Put one on, Maggie."

I looked at the rings and shook my head. "They're beautiful, but they're too big. They won't fit."

"Just put one on."

I picked up the gold ring and placed it on my finger. The band tingled, like a small charge of electricity was going through it, and it magically shrank to a perfect fit.

"Cool!" Raphael said. "Is the other one for me?"

"Sorry," Mr. McGuire said, looking sympathetically at Raphael. "I'm wearing the other."

"How come Maggie gets one, not me?"

"Because I'm his assistant!" I said, holding my hand out in front of his face.

"Geez," Raphael said, rolling his eyes. "I thought we'd moved past the whole *I'm a magician and you're not* thing. And here I was about to offer to be your trusty sidekick."

Mr. McGuire only smiled as he placed the other ring on his finger. Suddenly both opals glowed with a flickering green light. "I knew you'd want to come with me if I decided to confront Milo, so I brought these rings. As long as your opal continues to glow, you'll know I'm okay."

"But what if something does happen? How will I get to you?" I asked.

"You don't. You call Franny. I've written her number down on the folder here. Just tell her what we suspect, and she'll take it from there. And I won't take any unnecessary risks. I'll just go and ask Milo a few questions to make sure we're not unjustly accusing him of anything. If it turns out we're right, I'll let Viola Klemp handle the rest."

He looked up at the clock, took a deep breath, and smiled reassuringly at us. "I sincerely hope this is all a big misunderstanding and Milo's show will go on tonight as planned. But whatever happens, I'll be back by supper. Ask your grandmother to set an extra plate, and I'll supply the dessert."

"I really think you should let us come with you," I said once again.

"Don't worry, I can handle this," he said as he left the apartment.

I put my hand in the middle of the table and nervously drummed my fingers. Raphael glared at me, so I stopped, and the two of us just stared at the glowing opal.

"This waiting around and not knowing what's going on is making me crazy," I said after ten minutes had gone by. I clicked my fingernails on the table, matching the clock's rhythm. "Do you think he's there yet?" I asked, watching the green light glimmer and swirl in the stone.

"It should take around fifteen minutes to get to the part of town where Milo lives."

I jumped up and crossed the room to look out the window and clear my head. "He should've let us come with him."

Raphael walked over and sat on the edge of the coffee table. "Hey, Maggie. With all this talk about powers and levels, I was wondering, is Mr. McGuire more powerful than Milo? You know, in case they had to duke it out with wands or something."

"I don't know what level Mr. McGuire is—I only got to see him hold a meter stone and Milo wouldn't touch one in front of us. The stones give you a shock, so I thought he didn't want to get zapped in front of us, but maybe he just didn't want us to see what level it would show."

Suddenly the blood drained from my cheeks. "Oh no! Four magicians have disappeared and all of them were from this area. What if it was Milo? What if he figured out a way to steal their powers? That would explain how he mysteriously went from a level nineteen to a level thirty-eight. What if he keeps stealing powers? He could get so powerful, nobody could stop him."

"It's about time someone figured it all out!"

Hasenpfeffer called out from my room. Raphael's eyes grew wide. "Who is that?"

"Trouble," I said, running to Hasenpfeffer's cage. "Milo's behind the missing magicians, isn't he?"

Hasenpfeffer sat up on his haunches and nodded. "Brilliant deduction. And if you don't mind, I would appreciate it if you'd remove that spell you cast so I can get out of this prison. You really should get a book on rabbit care. This cage is terribly inadequate for my needs!"

"Whoa!" Raphael said from the doorway. "It talks."

"Yeah, too much—or in this case, not enough. Why didn't you tell me earlier?"

Hasenpfeffer sniffed. "Well, you didn't seem too interested in what I had to say *earlier*, and I wasn't sure you were trustworthy. I've only known you for a few days. Not to mention the fact I've been around humans long enough to know a rabbit has to look out for his own interests. One minute you discover you have a talking rabbit, the next, I'm the star attraction in some freak show, forced to entertain sniveling children poking their grimy fingers through my cage and—"

"Okay, I get it—rabbits are horribly mistreated . . ."

"And don't get me started about what happens to poor defenseless bunnies bought at Easter time. I weep when I start thinking about that—"

"Hasenpfeffer! Just tell us what you know about Milo," I interrupted. "Was I right? Is he stealing powers?"

He twitched his nose and hopped over to the cage door. "Lock first."

"Fine." I grabbed my wand and waved it over the cage. *"Tick tock goes the clock, tick tock undo the lock."*

The door swung open and Hasenpfeffer jumped out. He stretched his legs and scratched behind his ears. "Ooooh, yes," he said as he rolled around on his back and kicked his feet in the air. "That's better. My muscles were atrophying in there."

"What do you know about Milo?" I asked impatiently.

"Just about everything." He sat up and smoothed his fur with his paws. "It's funny, you'd think someone plotting all sorts of nasty business would do it in private. Yet Milo blathered on and on about all of his silly plans like I wasn't even there. But I suppose most magicians don't suspect their rabbits are listening. Really, when you think about it, most magicians never pay any attention to the rabbits once the show is over. We're the glue that holds the act together, the crowd-pleaser, and yet after the show is over, we're roundly ignored. Why I'd bet—"

"Look, Hasenpfeffer, can we talk about the plight of rabbits later? Mr. McGuire may be in trouble, and if you know something, we'd appreciate you filling us in."

"There, you see. You're a perfect example—rabbits are only important when you need something from them!"

"This is about Mr. McGuire being in serious danger!" I yelled.

"Did he always talk, or did you cast a spell on him?" Raphael asked, still staring wide-eyed at Hasenpfeffer.

"That's not important!"

"Actually, she did do it," Hasenpfeffer said to Raphael. "Right after she erased the memory of some monkey from her parents' minds."

"Can we get back to Milo?"

"You wiped out some of your parents' memories?" Raphael raised one eyebrow and took a step away from me.

"Let's stay focused here." I pointed to Hasenpfeffer. "Is Milo stealing powers or not?"

"Which one?" Hasenpfeffer asked. "The real Milo or his duplicate?"

"Either one!"

"Well, only the duplicate Milo is stealing powers."

"Fine, tell us about the duplicate, then."

"Well, when Milo copied himself, he assumed his twin would have the same powers he did. But the duplicate was a dud. And as an unwilling participant in the duplicate's feeble attempts at the simplest tricks, I can assure you his shows were a disaster. Milo was furious about the bad press his copy was getting. He was going to deep-six him, but Milo Two beat him to the punch! I don't know what happened to the original Milo." Hasenpfeffer narrowed his eyes. "One day there were two of them, the next, just one."

"But why did the twin start stealing powers?" Raphael asked.

Hasenpfeffer rolled his eyes. "He wanted to be like the original. He'd stolen some magic amplifier or amulet thingy to give his powers a boost, but it wasn't enough to pull off the caliber of tricks Milo usually did. Then he stumbled across a spell that stole powers from other magicians, and all of a sudden he's a big hit onstage. Everything was going smoothly until this duplicating spell he cast on me started to work—*a month after he cast it.* Oh, did he get flustered when I started multiplying during his rehearsal; it was really quite amusing."

"Mr. McGuire is probably walking into a trap!" I cried.

"But what kind of trap?" Raphael asked. "What happens to the magicians after their powers are stolen?"

"How should I know?" Hasenpfeffer said. "I spend most of my time confined to a cage. Speaking of which, perhaps we can move on to more important matters, such as a proper dwelling for myself? I have this absolutely *fabulous* plan for a new multilevel hutch and—"

"We'll deal with that later! We have to figure out how to warn Mr. McGuire. At least we know he's still okay." I held out my hand and suddenly noticed the opal in the ring was completely dark. "Raphael!" I screamed, shaking my hand in his face. "The ring! How long has it been black?"

"I don't know, I don't know! What do we do?" Raphael looked frantically around the room. "Where's the phone? We've got to call that lady."

We ran back to the kitchen and flipped through the papers until I found the folder with Franny's number. I raced for the phone, then stopped. "No," I said, calmly shaking my head. "I don't think she can do anything. She just raises animals; she doesn't have the power to fight Milo. And there may not be enough time. We have to go down to the shop."

"To the shop?" Raphael's mouth hung open. "Are you completely nuts? We're not supposed to go there, remember? Mr. McGuire said it might be dangerous, and I happen to agree with him." Relief washed over Raphael's face, and he put his hands on his hips. "Besides, I'm sure he always locks it when he leaves."

I took the extra shop key out of my pocket and

dangled it in front of his nose. "I had a feeling we might need this."

Raphael threw his hands up in the air. "Hello? Do the words 'poisonous snake' and 'man-eating lion' mean anything to you? This guy is out for blood." He picked up the telephone receiver and held it out. "I really think we ought to call that lady."

Part of me thought he was right; it would be great to call Franny and sit back and let someone else handle everything. But another part of me thought that I was pretty much responsible for a lot of the trouble that had happened, and if anyone was going to make the final repair on Milo the Magnificent, it was going to be me!

I folded my arms across my chest. "We're wasting time. Mr. McGuire's life may depend on us. Are you with me or not?"

Raphael looked at the phone in his hands and groaned. "Fine," he said, hanging it up. "But there'd better not be any more wild animals attacking us."

"Yeah, yeah. Now, let's get going. If you can get us across town, I think I know how we can stop Milo the Meathead."

"Hey, what about me?" Hasenpfeffer asked, hopping down the hall. "You'll need my help!"

I shook my head. "Sorry, we've got enough to deal with without worrying about you."

"But I know Milo. Maybe I can reason with him."

"Somehow I don't think Milo is interested in a rabbit reunion! I *wish* you were back in your *locked* cage!"

"This is the thanks I get?" Hasenpfeffer cried out from his cage in my room.

I grabbed a tote bag from the hall closet, then picked up a saltshaker from the table and tossed it in. "I hope there's enough salt in this thing in case Milo decides to send any more animals after us," I said as we headed for the door. "Let's get down to the shop—we have a mirror to break!"

19

Seven Years' Bad Luck

"You keep watch at the door while I get some more supplies," I said.

Raphael frowned, wrinkling his brow. "Do you really think it's such a good idea to break that mirror? I'll bet something like that is really, really expensive. Not to mention the seven years of bad luck you'll have coming."

"Mr. McGuire told me that I have to trust my intuition. I know this is what I have to do. It's just a feeling I have."

Raphael shook his head. "Yeah, well, your luck has

been pretty rotten so far. I can only imagine what the next seven years will be like."

"Your support is overwhelming." I took the jar of Magic Dust #4 off the shelf. "This is the last ingredient," I said as I poured a teaspoon into a container. I snapped the lid on and then put the container into a tote bag with a canister of salt I'd gathered. I went into the back room and looked at the mirror, which hadn't been covered up since we'd entered it earlier. I bit my lip and ran my fingers over the cool, dark glass, surprised it showed no reflection.

"Please let me be right about this," I said softly. "Raphael, can you find a hammer?" I asked louder.

Raphael came in and handed me a crowbar. "Is this okay? It was in his toolbox."

"I think it'll do the trick." I took a deep breath and stood in front of the mirror. "Get back." I covered my eyes with one arm, raised the crowbar over my head, and smashed the mirror.

Opening my eyes, I saw thick blue smoke curling up from the broken glass on the floor. I grabbed the blue sheet, ripped off a large piece, and carefully wrapped up a smooth, round chunk of glass about the size of a dinner plate. "I hope the spell will still work."

"What spell?" Raphael asked.

"The get-rid-of-the-creepy-duplicate-magician spell.

Now, let's catch the bus and get over to Milo's before Gram comes home and starts looking for me."

"You know, if Milo doesn't get us, my mom and your grandmother will. They're going to have a fit when they find out we went across town on a bus."

"I know, but we don't have a choice."

"*Yes, we do!*" Raphael said. "We can still call that lady."

"Fine. You call her, and I'll just go save Mr. McGuire myself." I stalked out of the back room and pulled Mr. McGuire's money box out from under the counter.

I could hear Raphael sigh. "I'm coming, I'm coming."

"How many tokens will we need?" I asked.

Raphael looked into the box, grabbed some tokens, and dropped them into a pocket of his overalls. "This is enough."

I put the box back and snatched the tote bag off the counter. "Let's do it!"

Raphael shook his head and followed me out the door to the bus stop.

"Here it comes," Raphael said, pointing down the block. The bus pulled up and squealed to a stop, and I groaned. The bus had a huge ad for Milo's shows under the windows.

"This is a bad sign," Raphael said, pointing at Milo's enormous gray eyes.

"Forget it. Let's just go."

Raphael took out the tokens and dropped them into the slot, then pointed to some empty seats near the back.

One look around at the crying babies and the people talking over the hum of the diesel engine, and I knew it was only a matter of time before my temples would begin to throb again. *The last thing I need is a headache*, I thought, as the pain grew with each bump. "I just *wish* these people would be quiet," I said aloud.

Instantly the bus was silent. I gaped at the other passengers now sitting serenely with their mouths closed. The bus driver looked back nervously in his mirror, and I wondered if he was expecting to see some trouble.

Raphael continued to look straight ahead, eyes wide. "Did you do that?" he whispered out of the corner of his mouth.

"I think so," I said quietly. "But I didn't mean to!"

"Can you undo it?"

"I think so." Quietly I muttered a new wish.

The driver checked his mirror again as the bus burst with lively chatter, punctuated with the loud cries of a baby.

Raphael gave me a sideways look. "That was interesting. And it might come in handy at school—you know, when Darcy starts in on you."

I nodded and looked out the window, watching the apartment buildings and storefronts give way to larger and larger homes.

"Maggie? Shouldn't we have a plan?"

"We'll know what to do when we get there."

"Oh, yeah, I forgot—your all-powerful intuition. Not that it warned you about the venomous snake or the lion."

I glared at him and then looked down at the dark opal on my finger.

"Do you think Mr. McGuire's okay?" Raphael asked. "I mean, you don't think he's . . . you know?"

"No. I think he's okay. He may be old, but he's tough."

Raphael nodded and I felt a little better until the bus rounded the corner and stopped. Raphael looked out the window. "This is where we get out."

I clutched the tote bag to my chest, and Raphael and I got off the bus. I looked at the tree-lined street with the big, beautiful houses and was struck by how clean and different it was from the street my grandmother lived on. "Oh no," I said. "I didn't write down the address! How are we going to figure out which house is his?"

Raphael took out a copy of Milo's magician's license from a pocket and waved it in the air. "I had a *feeling* this might come in handy."

I snatched the paper from his hand and looked at the address. "Okay, smart guy, where is 56 Oak Place?"

Raphael pointed down the street. "Even without the address, I recognize it from the pictures we saw."

My eyes followed Raphael's finger to a rambling lawn, scattered with tall oaks, leading up to a huge brick mansion at the end of a long driveway. The fence that surrounded the yard was topped with metal hats and rabbits where the spikes would ordinarily go. "Yeah, the fence is a dead giveaway."

As we neared the entranceway, Raphael stopped and tugged my arm back. "Okay, what does your intuition say about vicious guard dogs?" he asked, pointing to the five monster hounds prowling around the house.

I put the tote bag on the sidewalk. "Do you trust me?" I asked.

"Do I have a choice?"

"Put out your hands."

Raphael held out his hands, and I took out the container of salt.

"Salt? Wouldn't, like, dog biscuits be better?" he asked as I poured a pile out into his palms.

"We're not going to feed it to them—we're going to throw it at them. I'll bet they're magic, just like the lion. They'll disappear when the salt hits them."

Raphael raised his eyebrows.

"Do you have a better idea?"

Raphael shrugged. "You're in charge."

I poured some salt into one of my own hands and hooked the tote bag around my elbow. "Let's do it!"

I squeezed through the partly open gates, cringing as the metal hinges squeaked loudly. "Here we go," I whispered as the dogs' heads jerked up and looked our way. One dog let out a long, deep howl and led the other dogs bounding down the lawn.

"Get ready to throw the salt!" I yelled over the barking.

When the dogs got within three feet, I shouted, "Now!"

"What does your intuition tell you now?" Raphael hollered as the dogs ran through the salt and leapt at us.

"Run!"

20

Secrets in the Basement

Before I could even turn around, this huge hulk of a dog nailed me in the chest with its front paws and knocked me to the ground. If that wasn't bad enough, the thing sat on me like I was some sort of lawn chair. I had to turn my head to keep a gob of drool that was dripping out of its mouth from sliming my face, and I saw Raphael was pinned on his side.

"Okay, I was wrong. Any ideas?" I asked, struggling to breathe under the dog's weight.

Raphael gave a weak smile and rasped out, "They're mastiffs—I saw them on Animal Planet. They're trained to sit on intruders. We just need to show them who's boss. *Shoo!*" he yelled.

The dogs all pricked up their ears, then turned and ran around to the back of the house. "Wow, am I good or what?" Raphael asked as he stood up. "It's obvious they sensed I'm a dominant alpha-dog kinda guy."

"Uh," I said, relieved I could breathe again, "either that or they sensed he is." I got up, brushed the grass and dirt off the back of my shorts, and pointed toward the house. Raphael turned as Milo's chauffeur, Reginald, came around the corner with the dogs at his heels. As he came closer, we could see a gold whistle hanging around his neck.

"Dog whistle?"

"I think so," I said.

Raphael shrugged. "Can't blame a guy for trying."

"I've been waiting for you," Reginald said as he got close. "You're late. The Master thought you'd arrive with the old man."

"Um, we took a later bus, I guess," I said.

Reginald stared at us for a few seconds, then turned to the house. "Follow me."

"Should we go?" asked Raphael.

"Well, we wanted to get into the house," I said. The dogs growled, and we began walking. "Besides, I don't think we have a choice."

"He's got to be in the ninety-ninth percentile in height," Raphael whispered, pointing at Reginald. "And what's with the 'master' stuff?"

"I think he's a duplicate. He has the same gray eyes as Milo. But he seems to be missing something up here," I said, pointing to the side of my head.

We caught up to Reginald, who was standing frozen at the front door. We stood in silence and exchanged puzzled looks, waiting for him to open it.

"Why is he just standing there?" Raphael whispered.

"I don't think he knows what to do." I looked up into Reginald's blank face, then reached up and tapped him on the shoulder. "Excuse me, but you'll have to turn the knob to let us in."

Reginald turned to me and smiled. "Yes, you're quite right! Thank you." He opened the door and, after sending the dogs away, ushered us in. "Let me think," Reginald said. "Are you to go into the parlor or the library?" He looked into the two rooms on either side of the entryway and scratched his head.

Raphael sniffed and wrinkled his nose. "It doesn't smell very good in here. Doesn't Milo believe in air fresheners?"

"Wow, check this out—look how red it is," I said as we walked through the entryway. I ran my fingers along the soft red velveteen wallpaper.

"Look at all of the pictures of Milo," Raphael said. "There must be hundreds of them. The guy is totally in love with himself."

"Someone redecorating, Reginald?" I asked, pointing to the strips of red paper that had been torn off and left crumpled over a pile of broken picture frames.

"Yes, the Master said it's time for a change. He much prefers purple these days." He stared at me, and then his eyes lit up. "Oh, yes, I remember now. I'm to lock you in the basement with the others. You're to wait there until the Master gets home and can siphon off your powers."

A chill ran up my spine. "I hope we're not too late," I whispered.

Reginald chewed on the top of his thumb. "I don't think I was to mention that. I would be most grateful if you would refrain from telling the Master I let you in on his plan."

Reginald looked like a big puppy dog about to get swatted with a rolled-up newspaper, and I had a feeling I could use his fear to our advantage. "Sure, no problem, big guy. It'll be our little secret."

Reginald clapped his hands together. "Oh, thank you!" He smiled at me like I was his new best friend. "Now, if you'll follow me, please."

I winked at Raphael. "That's okay. We know the way."

Reginald looked totally confused and opened his mouth to say something, but nothing came out.

"It's like this," I continued. "We ran into Milo on our way over."

Reginald's dull eyes widened.

I smiled. "I know, I know, we thought he was at his show too, but it turns out he decided to take a, uh, a *train ride* instead—you know—choo, choo. Anyway, he told us to lock ourselves in the basement while you pick him up at the station." I held my wrist out and showed him my watch. "Oh my, it's getting late. You'd better move along."

"Yeah, and if he's late," added Raphael, "he said you need to wait for him. No matter how long it takes."

Reginald stared at us. Deep creases appeared on his forehead as he gnawed on a fingertip. "But—I—thought," he said, and pursed his lips. "No. I'm to wait here until the show is over so I can guard you."

"Oh, I almost forgot," I said, "Barty Bananas will be there too! He and Milo are going to have dinner after their train ride and they want *you* to come."

Reginald gasped. "*Me?* Barty Bananas asked *me* to come for dinner?"

"Yes," I said. "He heard you were a big fan. We weren't supposed to tell you, but Barty said you're the guest of honor!"

"Oh!" Reginald clapped his hands again. "I'm his *biggest* fan! I better hurry; I don't want to keep Barty waiting! Do I look okay?"

I wrapped my arm in Reginald's and led him to the front door. "You look fabulous! You're even wearing a bow tie—just like Barty! Be sure to give him our love, and do tell Milo I'm looking forward to having my powers sucked out. Don't forget, we need the keys so we can lock ourselves in the basement."

"Oh, yes, you're quite right," he said as he took a set of keys out of his pocket. He started to give them to me but hesitated and drew his hand back. "Are you sure the Master wants me to give you the keys?"

"Reginald," I said in a deep voice, wagging a finger at him. "I don't think Milo will be very pleased when I tell him how you're acting." I put one hand on my hip and held out an open palm. "And you know how much monkeys hate to wait."

Reginald dropped the ring of keys into my hand.

I gave him my biggest smile and opened the door. "Have fun, and don't eat too many bananas," I said as he walked out. I slammed the front door and turned the lock. "Can you believe that? He's completely nuts. The Lubchek twins are more on the ball than he is."

"What was wrong with him? He would've swallowed

a can of worms if we had told him Barty said to."

"Maybe something happened when he got duplicated. I'm just glad we ran into him instead of Milo."

"We better find Mr. McGuire and get out of here, fast!"

I jangled the keys. "Which way to the basement?"

Suddenly a loud crash from the room to our right made us both jump. "What was that?" I asked.

"Oh dear, not again!" someone called out.

"Who was that?" Raphael whispered.

We tiptoed over to the doorway and peeked in. A short woman dressed in a maid's uniform stood over a broken vase, nervously tapping her fingers on her chin.

"Dagmar?" I called out.

The woman turned to us and smiled, her dull eyes lighting up. "Yes, that's my name. Sometimes I forget, but now that you've said it, I'm sure that's it."

We walked into the library, careful to step around the shards of glass. "Duplicate alert," Raphael murmured.

I nodded, seeing a familiar pair of pale gray eyes peering out at us from under Dagmar's curly white hair. "Um, we need to go down to the basement. Can you point us in the right direction?"

Dagmar wrinkled her nose and frowned. "Oh, I'm

not allowed to go down there anymore. Pity, too, what with all those dusty people. I do think he should let me get at them. They really need a thorough going-over."

"Uh, that's okay. You don't have to go—just tell us where it is," I said.

"Goodness me. The basement is . . ." Dagmar paused and drummed her fingers on her chin again, trying to remember. "I think you need to go through the kitchen. I believe this way," she said, and pointed to a door at the back of the room. "Or is it the other way?"

"That's all right. We'll find it," I said. "Let's go, Raphael."

We started toward the door when Dagmar called out. "Pardon me," she said. "But are you going to get that nice man out of the basement, the one who has my cat?"

"Mr. McGuire?"

"Yes, that's his name. At least—I think it is."

"We're going to try."

"Oh, good. I'd hate to think of him getting all dusty and covered with cobwebs like the others."

"We'd better hurry, Raphael. I don't like the sound of that."

"Agreed," he said with a shiver. "Dusty people?"

We headed into a giant kitchen and I made a face. The stink coming from an overflowing garbage can was almost as bad as the cauldron.

"Ugh! Now we know why it smells in here," Raphael said, plugging his nose. "If I were Milo, I think I'd duplicate myself another maid. Dagmar's not doing a very good job."

"I think she's doing the best she can. I mean, she can't even remember her name."

I saw a door with a shiny new padlock on it. "That must lead to the basement."

"Hurry up and open it," Raphael said.

I looked at the key chain and groaned. "These are the keys to some house in Vienna," I said, showing Raphael a small label attached to the key ring. "That Neanderthal gave us the wrong keys!" I shook the lock and threw the keys on the counter. "What are we going to—oh, wait." I rolled my eyes and took my wand out of my back pocket. "I *wish* the lock would open."

The lock clicked, and I turned to Raphael. "I've spent so many years trying not to use my wish magic, I some-times forget to even try."

I took the lock off the doorjamb and slowly opened the door. I peered down the stairs, feeling around for a light switch.

"It's awfully quiet. Don't you think Mr. McGuire should be yelling for help or something?" Raphael asked.

"Maybe his mouth is taped up."

We walked to the bottom of the stairs and peeked around the corner. Colorful wooden props from old shows were piled everywhere—all covered with cobwebs. "Dagmar was right," I whispered. "This place does need a good dusting." I squinted into the dark corners. "Hey, see if you can find another light."

"I've got it," Raphael said, turning on a dim bulb. "Maggie, look!" Raphael jumped back, slamming into me.

I turned and felt my lunch churn and rise in my stomach. Three bodies were propped up against the wall like boards of wood, covered with at least half an inch of dust. My eyes traced the spiderwebs crisscrossing their noses and ears. I swallowed hard as a black spider pounced on a large fly in the webbing draped across Milo the Magnificent's open mouth.

"Now we know where the real Milo is," I said, backing away, my legs feeling wobbly.

"And Dagmar and Reginald." Raphael craned his neck forward, trying to get a better look without getting too close. "Are they—uh—dead?"

"I don't think so. I mean, besides the cobwebs, they look okay." I put down the tote bag and walked up to Milo. With a shaking hand I reached out and touched his wrist. "He's pretty cold, but not dead cold," I said, exhaling. "They must be under some sort of spell." I pulled a string of cobwebs from my hand and shook it off. "Mr. McGuire?" I called out quietly.

I moved some old posters aside and peeked around a bookshelf. Raphael walked over toward some empty birdcages.

"Maggie," Raphael said in a shaky voice, "how many magicians did you say were missing?"

"Four, I think."

"Well, I think I know what happens after someone steals your powers."

I walked over and saw two top hats lying next to a diamond tiara and a jester's hat. "Roland the Rainbow Magician," I said. I picked up the hat, and the small bells on the end of each point jingled. "He was the last one to disappear."

"Not the hats," Raphael said, pointing farther into the room. "There."

My eyes followed his finger, and I made out four long shapes lying partially covered under a sheet. I squinted and saw what appeared to be a mummified hand clutching a rainbow-striped wand.

"Oh my God," I whispered. I put the hat down and backed away from the bodies. "We need to find Mr. McGuire and get out of here—now!"

"Maggie, look! It's Mr. McGuire!" Raphael cried. "We're too late!"

21

On Ice

Mr. McGuire sat slumped in a chair. His head hung back over the top, and his arms dangled loosely at his side.

I sucked in a ragged breath as hot tears stung my eyes. "No! We can't be too late. We just can't!"

Mr. McGuire sat up with a start, knocking his glasses into his lap. "Huh? What's going on?" A look of relief passed over his face. "Oh, it's you two," he said, rubbing his eyes. "I must have fallen asleep."

I was so happy to see he was okay, I ran toward him. "We thought you were—"

"Stop!" he yelled. "Don't come any closer. Milo has me booby-trapped. He cast a containment spell around me. If anyone crosses the zone, we'll both get zapped."

"Zapped?" I asked, stopping in my tracks.

"'Zapped into oblivion' is what our counterfeit friend said. It's actually a rather interesting spell. Started out with a large fire snake that circled around me, and then—well, I guess it's not important." He placed his glasses on his nose and leaned forward in the chair. "I don't suppose you called Franny?" he asked, though I was sure he already knew the answer.

"I didn't think we had time."

"I told her to call, but she wouldn't listen," Raphael added.

"Never mind that—how did you get stuck down here?" I asked.

"Milo and Reginald were waiting for me." Mr. McGuire sighed. "Apparently he has a crystal ball that he's been using to keep tabs on us. After you noticed his eyes were the same color as the duplicate bunnies, he was afraid you'd put two and two together and expose him. He rigged that magic book in an attempt to scare you and keep you away from the shop."

"Scare me? He could've killed me," I said, glancing back at the real Milo, wondering if he was anything like his duplicate.

"He doesn't seem to have much of a conscience," Mr. McGuire said, shaking his head. "He was the one who cast the disfigurement spell on Franny after he froze the original Milo, along with Reginald and Dagmar."

"And those other magicians," Raphael said, furrowing his brow. "He got them, too."

Mr. McGuire bowed his head and nodded. "Fortunately, Milo was in a rush to get to his show, or I'm afraid I'd have suffered the same fate."

"Hasenpfeffer filled us in a little," I said. "I kind of cast a spell on him without knowing it. He can talk."

"Boy, can he talk!" Raphael added.

"Magic rabbits are highly suggestible," Mr. McGuire said. "I should have warned you."

"He told us Milo Two took the amplifiers from that witch."

"Yes, as I was escorted to the basement, he couldn't resist boasting about the whole affair. He told me he stole the magic amplifiers from Bruce. That increased his power enough to freeze the original Milo and stash him here in the basement."

"But what about Reginald and Dagmar? Why them?" Raphael asked.

"After the duplicate hid Milo in the basement, he copied the house staff before they could figure out what was going on and alert the authorities. As a matter of fact, I believe Dagmar's cat must have short-circuited the spell the first time he tried it. Instead of Dagmar being duplicated, Otto turned yellow. When the Milo duplicate did succeed in copying them, the magic was so diluted, the spell didn't work like it should have. The new Reginald and Dagmar are little more than trained seals."

I nodded. "We noticed that. But how did Franny get mixed up in this?"

"Milo Two knew he couldn't keep performing—he just didn't have enough power. And he needed a source of income."

"But you and Franny said Milo was, like, megarich."

"Apparently the real Milo spends his money as fast as he can make it. The duplicate found he'd be penniless in a very short time, so he hoped he could earn a living selling magic rabbits. But that botched rabbit-duplicating spell and Franny's refusal to purchase any left him out of luck. If he hadn't discovered that power-stealing spell, he probably would have slipped into obscurity. Unfortunately, we now have a rather powerful magician to contend with."

"So what should we do?" asked Raphael.

"We need to get the real Milo up and going."

"How?" I asked.

"Well, that's the question," Mr. McGuire said. "While

the duplicate was very forthcoming about most of his exploits, he never said what spell he used to freeze Milo. He may have feared I'd escape, and didn't want to give me the means to free Milo before he got back."

Mr. McGuire stood up and peered over at the three bodies, clucking his tongue. "I'm afraid I won't be much help trapped in here." He shook his head. "You'll have to do the legwork for this repair job, Maggie. Poke around the bodies for any clues."

I groaned.

Raphael took a giant step back. "Gee, it's too bad I'm not a magic guy, otherwise I'd love to give you a hand."

"Oh, I don't want to have all the fun. Besides, you're my trusty sidekick, remember? You get to help too." I tugged on Raphael's sleeve and pulled him toward Milo.

"Did I say I wanted to be a sidekick?" Raphael asked as I dragged him over. "What I really had in mind was more like a cheerleader. You know—go, Maggie! Go check out those dusty people!" He looked at me hopefully, weakly punching the air with his fists. "Rah? Rah?"

"Too late for that. You're part of the team." I held my breath and flapped Milo's cape a few times, shaking some of the spiders off. "What are we looking for?" I asked, turning my head away from the cloud of dust floating in the air.

"A spell like this often needs some sort of conduit—something to channel the magic through and keep it in place," Mr. McGuire called out. "If I'm right, all three of them will probably have some sort of matching pin on their clothing or perhaps an amulet or gemstone. Remove the conduit and the spell is broken."

I grimaced as I turned to face Milo and the others. "Let's just get started. You take Dagmar and I'll check out Milo and Reginald. Let's do this together—starting at the top."

Raphael stood on tiptoes. "At the top we have one goofy maid's hat and cobwebby white hair."

"And Milo has one red velvet hat and greasy, cobwebby black hair," I said, teetering on my toes. "I don't see any pins or anything stuck in his hat, just a few spiders. Reginald has . . ." I jumped up in front of the chauffeur a few times. "One chauffeur's hat and one monster-size head. Milo has a gold clasp on his cape, but Reginald just has regular buttons on his jacket."

"Ditto for Dagmar—just plain buttons."

I crouched down and scanned the three sets of shoes. "I don't see anything unusual."

"The charm could be as insignificant as a straight pin," Mr. McGuire said. "I think it may be time to start a more thorough search."

"I wonder if Milo wears velvet underwear?" Raphael asked.

"I so don't want to know," I said, curling my lip in disgust. I took a step back, tracing every detail of the bodies with my eyes. "You know, something just isn't right about this. I feel like I'm missing something."

A large wolf spider crawling out from Milo's collar caught my eye. I shuddered as it made its way up toward his forehead. "Hey, their hats!"

"Hats?" Raphael asked.

"Their hats would have fallen off when Milo Two brought them down to the basement. Why would he go out of his way to put them back on instead of dumping them with the other ones?"

I stretched my arm up to grab Milo's hat. "Oh," I cried as my hand went right through the brim. "It's not real." I grabbed the saltshaker out of the tote bag. "Let's see if this has any effect." I poured some salt in my palm, then flung the salt up at Milo. The hat shimmered and smoldered, disappearing in a cloud of yellow smoke.

"Hey, the salt did come in handy!" Raphael said.

"Do you see anything on his head?" Mr. McGuire called out.

I pulled an old chair over to Milo and stood up on it. "There's this tiny snowflake—it's about the size of a dime. It looks like it's made out of ice, too! It's attached to some sort of clip."

Mr. McGuire nodded and smiled appreciatively. "Magic ice. Now that *is* clever. I wouldn't have thought of using that to freeze someone. Whatever this twin lacks in the morals department, he certainly makes up for in his ability to find unique spells."

"Hey," I said, "don't I get any credit for finding the magic ice?"

Raphael clapped his hands together a few times. "I'll give you all the credit you want. Let's just get out of here before he uses the ice on any of us."

"Okay, you need to remove the conduit. But make sure you don't touch it!" Mr. McGuire warned. "*Just* the clip."

I reached out and tried to squeeze open the clasp attached to the flake. "Ow! It burned my hand! I thought it was supposed to be cold."

"Another booby trap," Mr. McGuire said. "You'll have to see if you can break the spell on the clip. Or maybe use a spell to melt the snowflake."

I blew on my hand and frowned. "I have an easier solution. I *wish* I had a pair of scissors."

A pair of round-tipped kindergarten scissors appeared in my hand. "Probably not the best for cutting hair, but it should do the trick." I leaned in and grabbed a big chunk of hair, and had to make at least twenty cuts with the dull scissors until the clip dropped to the floor and the snowflake shattered.

"Let's hope he's so grateful we rescued him, he doesn't mind the bad haircut," I said, hopping off the chair and putting the scissors down.

"Uh, guys, isn't he supposed to be moving or something?" Raphael asked.

Mr. McGuire frowned. "I was afraid of this. He's been frozen for quite some time—I fear he may need a little jump start to get going."

"Jump start?" I asked.

Mr. McGuire smiled weakly at me. "You just need to reach inside him and give his heart a couple of squeezes."

Raphael shuddered all over. "Excuse me? Did you say 'reach inside him'?" he asked, covering his chest with his hands.

"It's not quite as bad as it sounds. It's a matter of drawing out his essence, Maggie. It will look just like Milo; only it will be transparent, like a ghost. Then you need to reach into it and get the heart going. Once Milo's spirit is reunited with his body, he'll wake up."

"No," I said, backing away from Milo. "This is too much—I'm not ready for something like this!"

"But you are, Maggie. You can do it. I'll talk you through the procedure."

"I don't know if I can do it. I mean, taking hold of someone's spirit? It just doesn't seem possible."

Raphael smiled. "If anyone can draw out someone's spirit and grab hold of their heart, it's you. And I think it would be in our best interest to be outta here before Milo Two gets back. Besides," he said, punching me lightly in the arm, "I have this *feeling* you can do it."

"Thanks, I think." I sighed and turned to Milo. "Okay, what's first?"

"Put your hands on Milo's shoulders," Mr. McGuire said.

I brushed some of the dust lingering on the red velvet cape and placed my hands on his shoulders. "Now what?"

"Now concentrate; try to feel some spark of life. When you do, keep your fingers clenched and slowly back up. If you've gotten a good hold, his essence should pull out with you."

I looked up into Milo's frozen face and grasped his shoulders harder. My fingers began to tingle and I started to back up. As I stepped back, I felt something tugging on my fingers, keeping me from moving. "I can't budge it—it won't come out," I said through clenched teeth.

"Keep concentrating," Mr. McGuire said. "It isn't going to be easy; the spirit doesn't like to leave the body."

"Just think about what that phony Milo did to us," Raphael said.

I thought about Franny's boils and Raphael's magic show. I thought about Dagmar's and Reginald's duplicates wandering around like little kids. Feeling the anger well up inside me, I narrowed my eyes and yanked at Milo's shoulders, finally falling backward with his spirit held dangling from my fingers. I stood up and held the paper-light essence up to the light. "Yuck! It feels sticky like the cobwebs."

"Yuck is right," Raphael said, staring at the filmy thing in my hands. "You magic guys have all the fun," he said, turning away. "He's all yours, Mags. Get this guy going!"

I pursed my lips and held the spirit up with one hand. "What's next?"

"Reach inside the chest area," Mr. McGuire said. "Everything will feel cold inside, except his heart. You'll need to grab hold of it and give it a couple of good squeezes to get it going again. Once you feel it beating, touch the spirit to Milo's body and he should revive."

Slowly I reached inside Milo's spirit and began to shiver. "Cold? It's like the Arctic inside this thing." My teeth chattered as I fished my hand inside, feeling for the heart. "It isn't where it should be. I don't feel anything warm."

"Try down by his stomach, Maggie," Mr. McGuire said. "It may have settled a bit."

I reached down and yelped, grabbing onto what felt like a big warm muffin. I squeezed it twice, and the heart jumped to life in my hands, spreading its warmth through the spirit. I took my hand out, picked up the other shoulder, and walked toward Milo's body. The spirit was ripped from my fingers as soon as it touched his body. Milo's cheeks flushed and the magician staggered forward, sputtering and coughing.

"At the very least, my idiot twin could have closed my mouth after he froze me," Milo gasped as he stood up stiffly. He looked down at his vest and screeched in horror at the spider crawling across his chest. "Get it off!" he bellowed.

I ran over and brushed the small black spider off Milo's chest, and jumped back as he jerked around in a circle, quickly examining his clothing for more spiders. "I loathe insects," he said when he got himself back together.

"Spiders aren't actually insects—they're aracⱢids," I said.

Milo glowered at me, wrinkling his nose as if I were a spider. "And pray tell, who might you be?" he asked.

"I'm Maggie, and this is Raphael. Mr. McGuire is over there stuck in the chair."

Milo surveyed us and nodded at Mr. McGuire. "I've heard of you, McGuire. You run a repair shop, if I'm not mistaken. Would someone be so kind as to tell me today's date?"

"September third," I said.

"For pity's sake!" roared Milo. "I am surrounded by imbeciles! I've been rotting in this moldy basement covered with spiders, and it has taken you addle-brained ninnies over two months to find me?"

I stared in disbelief at Milo. "What's wrong with *us*? We've risked our necks trying to find you! How about a thank-you?"

"Thank-you? For what?" Milo leaned down, breathing stale breath in my face. "For leaving me to waste away in this basement? For letting that fraud continue to perform substandard shows that have probably destroyed my career?"

"Wait a minute," I said. "You made the duplicate in the first place; we were only trying to help."

"And we just rescued you," Raphael added.

"And I think you should show some appreciation," Mr. McGuire said from his chair. "You would've been trapped in this basement for goodness knows how long if Maggie and Raphael hadn't come."

Milo scowled at the three of us, nostrils flaring, then calmly brushed some of the dust off his cape. "Yes," he said, taking a deep breath, "it is a very sad state of affairs when one has to be rescued by an old man and two smart-mouthed children. And I see you allowed yourself to be locked up in a containment spell. Looks like he used one of my favorites! Tsk, tsk," he said, wagging a finger at Mr. McGuire. "Must be more careful. I suppose you'll be wanting me to lift it off, eh?"

"That would be appreciated," Mr. McGuire said angrily as red splotches erupted on his face.

"As you wish." He reached into his cape and withdrew a bloodred wand. He circled the wand in Mr. McGuire's direction. *"Circle of harm, fire snake, hear my words and make a break."* He flicked the wand once and a flaming, winged snake appeared at Mr. McGuire's feet. It flew up and around him until it finally dove into the ceiling, leaving a circular scorch mark behind. Milo waved his hand with a flourish as he bowed. "Happy now?" he asked, hands folded on his chest.

"Yes, thank you," Mr. McGuire said, waving the thin wafts of smoke away from his face. He pushed his sleeves up roughly and walked toward Milo. "I do think you owe us an apology. The duplicate you created has caused us a great deal of trouble."

Milo opened his eyes, round and innocent like a baby's. "How can I possibly be held responsible for the things my duplicate did while I was out of commission?

And really, I can't be blamed for trying to enrich the world with two of me. Who knew my twin would be a dud? Why," he said, palms outstretched, "it hardly seems possible."

"A monkey would've realized making a copy of him would be a rotten idea," Raphael whispered to me.

Milo spun toward Raphael, jabbing his wand into his chest. "I heard that, young man!" Milo shouted. "I'd be careful if I were you."

"Now, see here!" Mr. McGuire huffed, drawing Raphael safely to his side. "I've had enough of you and your self-important babble. You have an evil duplicate running amok, and, if I'm not mistaken, you'll be in need of our assistance to make him disappear. You may have had the power and the misguided ego to make the duplicate, but you don't have the power to get rid of him. Your duplicate has stolen the power of at least four magicians. If he keeps at it, we may never be able to stop him!"

"Stolen powers? How intriguing," Milo said, excitedly tapping his fingers together, his blue eyes gleaming. "Perhaps I misjudged him. How ever did he do it?" he asked sweetly.

"Like we'd tell you," I said with a snort.

"Enough!" shouted Mr. McGuire. "The duplicate's show is almost over, and he may already realize we're free.

We need to get to the Black Rock School and get rid of that impostor *now*! Are you going to cooperate with us or not?" Mr. McGuire put his hands on his hips and raised his eyebrows. "And, I might add, the only other magic repairman with the means to assist you currently lives on the coast of Scotland."

Milo threw up his hands. "If I must mingle with the rabble, so be it. I am at your mercy, kind sir. What are we to do?" he asked, his voice dripping with honey.

"We need to get a mirror and some magic powders from my shop. I only hope we have enough time to get to the school before he leaves."

"Uh, Mr. McGuire," I said, biting my lip. "I had a feeling we'd need that stuff, so we brought it with us. That is, we brought the powders and a piece of the mirror. I didn't know how to take the whole thing with us, so I kind of broke it." I took out the wrapped-up shard of glass from the tote bag and held my breath as I gave it to him.

"Kinda broke it," Raphael said, eyes wide. "Kinda smashed it to a million pieces is more like it."

"No, Maggie, it's perfect," Mr. McGuire said, hugging me. "And it will make transporting it much easier."

"Bravo for Maggie," Milo said, rolling his eyes. "If we have this *mirror*, we should be off. I feel quite ill at ease knowing that fraud is out and about. Why don't you hurry and free up these other two, McGuire."

"Actually," Mr. McGuire said, "Maggie and I will both do it. She's the one who freed you."

Milo ran his fingers along his mustache and gave me a smile that sent chills down my spine. "My, my. A miniature magician. This all just gets more interesting by the minute. Well, when you *two* are done, Reginald can take us to the theater in one of my cars."

22

Family Reunion

As we walked down the hall to the auditorium, I could hear people clapping.

"Performing in an *elementary school*," Milo muttered bitterly. "It will be an uphill battle to get my career back on track."

"This way," Raphael said, leading us through the stage door.

While Mr. McGuire got the mirror and the powders ready, Raphael and I peeked out from behind a curtain to see what Milo Two was doing. The duplicate had just levitated a huge metal safe high above his head. He waved his wand in circles, and the safe twirled, spinning faster and faster, letting off a cascade of fireworks.

"If we're lucky, he'll drop it on himself," I said.

I watched his assistant wave a sequined hand above her head as the safe's door swung open. A flock of white doves flew out and circled the audience twice, then disappeared in puffs of brightly colored confetti that showered down to great applause.

"That was actually pretty cool, don't you think?" I turned to Raphael and paled. "Oh no! Pip!"

Raphael looked down just as Pip jumped out of his front pocket and scurried onto the stage.

"You've had Pip with you this whole time?"

Raphael gaped after her as she made her way toward Milo. "I thought she might be traumatized after being in that hat and didn't want to leave her alone."

"Well, do something before Milo sees her!"

Raphael started toward the stage.

"Are you crazy?" I whispered through clenched teeth. I grabbed his sleeve and yanked him back.

The two of us watched Pip sniff her way to the edge of the stage. Darcy Davenport, who was sitting in the front row next to her mother, pointed.

Mrs. Davenport jumped up in her seat. "Mouse!" she shrieked, waving her hands in the air.

Milo Two jerked his head toward the audience and the safe came crashing down, splintering the stage inches from his assistant, who then rushed off.

"I *wish* Pip were invisible," I called out too late as she scrambled off the lip of the stage into the orchestra pit.

"Pip!" Raphael hollered, running out after her.

"You!" roared Milo Two. "What are you doing here?"

Not waiting for a reply, he pointed his wand at Raphael. *"Soar like the birds, buzz like the flies, I command this boy to up and rise!"*

Raphael cried out as he flew into the air high above the stage, stunning the audience into silence.

"That's Raphael!" Nahla Jackson cried out.

"Levitating," Sal Perez said.

Milo Two peered into the wings and smiled. "Where there's one rat, the others aren't far behind. You'd best come out before I dash this annoying pest to the floor."

I stared at Raphael spinning in the air high over my head. My first instinct was to turn and run, but Raphael was covering his eyes, moaning, and I remembered the words on the repair shop sign.

With magic comes responsibility.

"This is my repair job," I whispered, "and I'm going to take care of it!"

Taking a deep breath, I took my wand out of my tote

bag and walked onto the stage, hoping I could distract Milo Two until Mr. McGuire and the real Milo had the mirror ready to go.

Milo Two turned to the audience and bowed. "For my grand finale, I will make my two young assistants disappear—forever!"

"Not before I get to do my trick," I said, pointing my wand at Milo Two. *"Need a new place for the roaches to roam, let your silly grape cape be their new home!"*

Hundreds of giant cockroaches scurried out from under the duplicate's purple cape, swarming over his body, and spilling out onto the stage. The magician howled and shrieked, swatting them away.

Mr. McGuire ran out with the mirror. "Now!" he called.

On cue, the real Milo walked slowly onto the stage. "This is where it ends, you incompetent fraud."

Milo Two froze momentarily, eyes wide with surprise. With an evil slash of a smile, he stood straight and tall, and waved his wand over his head. The roaches all jumped off and darted into the dark corners of the stage. Milo Two looked back at me and shook his head. "You merely caught me off guard. I'm not nearly as fearful of insects as he is."

Straightening his cape, he walked over to Milo with a cold smile. "So, you're back. Miss me?"

"Why, you cheeky impostor!" Milo slapped his

duplicate, sending his purple top hat skidding across the stage. "Where's that mirror, McGuire?"

Mr. McGuire uncovered the piece of glass, blew on the magic dust, and pointed it toward Milo.

Milo Two calmly took a few steps back. "Ah, the uneducated are so tiresome," he said, shaking his head in disgust. "Didn't you bother to read the mirror's instruction manual? I did. I found it on your shelves while Maggie was droning on and on about her pathetic little wishes. I thought some research was in order after that rabbit fiasco. Unlike those bunnies, human copies aren't so easily drawn into the mirror. As a matter of fact, someone would have to forcibly shove me into the mirror. But I can see you didn't know that, McGuire. You really should keep up with your reading."

Milo Two turned toward me. "I read another interesting tidbit too." He sprang, pouncing on me like a spider, wrapping an arm tight across my neck. He spun back to face Mr. McGuire and Milo. "If I'm in contact with another person when I'm forced into the mirror, they come too. *Permanently*."

"No!" My heart raced as I thrashed around, trying to break free. "Let me go!"

He tightened his hold across my neck. I gasped for air as I kicked my heels back into his legs.

"Relax, Maggie. If we play our cards right, neither one of us will be going into that mirror." I stopped struggling and the duplicate relaxed his grip. "That's a good girl."

Mr. McGuire headed toward us, but the duplicate held out his other hand and I could hear the audience whispering about the turn of events.

"Perhaps you should all just walk to the other side of the stage, and let me and my friend leave the theater. And I might remind you: I've amassed quite a bit of power. I could snuff Maggie out in a heartbeat if any of you feel the need to start casting spells."

Milo Two looked at Milo standing at the opposite end of the stage and sighed. "We could have done so much together. We could have been unstoppable. You just couldn't stand the fact that your mirror image was imperfect." He walked toward the steps leading down into the audience, pulling me along. "But I've outgrown you, Milo. I've become so much more. Of course, adding Maggie's powers to my own will just be the icing on the cake."

He brought his free hand to his lips and blew Milo a kiss. "Until we meet again, brother."

"Oh, that is it!" Milo roared. He turned to Mr. McGuire and yanked the mirror from his hands. "He's going in, and I don't care if the girl goes with him!"

"No," I pleaded. My eyes grew wide as Milo stormed across the stage, the mirror raised over his head.

"I've a confession," Milo Two whispered in my ear as I struggled to get away. "The powers I steal don't last. I used just about everything up doing the show. It was all a bluff." He chuckled crazily. "Looks like we're going in after all."

"He's powerless!" I hollered. "Don't do it!" I kicked wildly as Milo charged toward us. "Stop! Please!" I begged, remembering the awful creatures in the mirror.

"Milo, no!" Mr. McGuire yelled, running toward him.

"This is it, Margaret," Milo Two said sadly. "I'll just disappear, but you'll be living the rest of your life in the bowels of the mirror."

I twisted frantically, hot tears running down my face. "Let go of me!" I shrieked as Milo got closer.

"Maggie, level fifty!" Raphael yelled out from some-where above the stage. *"Level fifty!"*

Suddenly I understood. I stared at the other side of the stage and yelled, *"I wish I was there!"* I felt my body wrenched from Milo Two's arms and in a flash found myself on the other side of the stage. Dizzy and nauseous, I struggled to stay upright.

Across the stage Mr. McGuire dove into the back of Milo's legs, just as he was bringing the mirror down on top of the duplicate's head. Knees buckling, Milo collapsed backward as Mr. McGuire belly flopped and skidded across the floor. Milo Two fell on top of Milo, and, as the mirror flashed, I could see the pure pleasure in the duplicate's gray eyes as he dragged his creator into the mirror. Milo's screams echoed through the theater as the fragment clattered to the floor.

There was a moment of silence, and then the audience broke into wild applause.

"Close the curtain!" Mr. McGuire called to a confused stagehand as he staggered to his feet. "Close the curtain!"

I ran to Mr. McGuire, pulling him back as the curtain crashed down in front of us. "Raphael!" I cried. "Where is he?"

"I'm up here."

I looked up and let out a sigh. Raphael sat on a catwalk high above our heads. "Once he grabbed you, he stopped paying attention," he called down. "I just kept floating up, and when I reached one of these walkways, I climbed on. The view's pretty good."

Suddenly Gram pushed her way through the curtains and hugged me tightly. "Maggie, are you all right?"

"Gram!" I said, pulling away. "How did you know we were here?"

"When you weren't at the apartment when I got home, I tried the shop. And then when I still couldn't find you, I checked with Mrs. Santos, who said she hadn't seen Raphael since she'd sent him out to clean up the things from his magic show. I offered to come to the school to check and see if you two had gone to the benefit show without telling us. What I wasn't expecting was to see you vanish from one end of the stage and then reappear on the other the minute I walked in."

"That was Maggie being a level fifty magician!" Raphael said.

Gram stared at me, dumbfounded. "Magician? You . . ."

I nodded. "Gram, I'm like Grandpa. I can do magic." I looked up at Raphael and shook my head. "And if Raphael hadn't called out 'level fifty,' I'd be stuck in that mirror too."

"Hey, I figured it was statistically possible you could be a level fifty and worth a shot."

"Level fifty?" Gram said, putting her hand to her chest.

"I was going to tell you," I said.

"Let's talk about this at your apartment, where we'll have more privacy," Mr. McGuire said wearily, smoothing his hair. "And I'll need to report this to Viola Klemp."

"Hey," Raphael called out as he climbed down the last rung of a ladder and dropped to the stage. "What about Pip? We can't leave her here!"

"I'll handle this," I said. "A friend of mine taught me a spell for conjuring mice at a magic show I attended." I walked to center stage and picked up the purple velvet hat lying there. Waving my wand over the hat's opening, I chanted, *"Hibbity, jibbity, ribbity, zip; when I tap it three times, out comes Pip!"* I tapped the rim, and Pip poked her pink nose out.

"Pip! You're safe," Raphael cried as he scooped her up.

Gram put her arms around me again and squeezed tight.

"Hey, you all have to see this," Raphael called out.

I turned. Raphael was standing by the curtain, holding the mirror fragment.

As I got closer, I could hear muffled shouting coming from the glass.

"McGuire! Get me out of here!"

I looked in the mirror and gasped. There was Milo the Magnificent, his red cape flapping around in the swirling fog. He shook his fist and pounded on his side of the mirror, shrieking.

"I'll get you for this!" he hollered. "I'll make you all pay horribly!" He stopped, staring into the unending mist.

When he glanced up again, I thought he might be crying. "McGuire? Are you out there?" he called miserably.

Mr. McGuire took the shard from Raphael. "I'm here, Milo."

"It's not true what he said, is it? It can't be true. Please tell me I'm not trapped here forever?"

"I don't know," Mr. McGuire said quietly.

Milo turned to me, and I shuddered as his eyes hardened into small dark balls of hate. "You," he snarled. "I have a little advice for you. The world of magic is a dangerous place. If you decide to cultivate this little talent of yours, watch your back. For every magician like Mr. McGuire, there are at least a hundred like me. And one way or another, I'll see you get your comeuppance." He slammed into the glass, clawing at it. "Just you wait!"

A crop of goose bumps popped up on my arms as Milo threw himself against the glass over and over again. Suddenly the mist in the mirror was alive with gray, snaky shadows—Milo screamed, thrashing at the creatures. A wave of fog blew across the glass, and he was gone.

"It was real—all of it," came a breathless voice behind us.

I jumped around and saw Fiona staring at us with wide eyes.

"It wasn't a trick," she said. "That man is *really* in the mirror, and you . . ."

I shook my head. "No! It's not what you think."

She pointed to me. "It was you all along, wasn't it? Everything at school. You made it happen."

"Fiona, just let me explain."

Her bottom lip quivered. "I thought you were my friend."

"Wait! I am your friend. I was trying to help you," I yelled as Fiona turned and ran off the stage.

My shoulders slumped as Mr. McGuire picked up the blue cloth lying in the middle of the stage and wrapped the mirror up tightly. "I think," he said wearily, "it's time to go. We have *a lot* to talk about."

23

Family Ties

I stood on the ladder in the repair shop and picked a jar off the shelves. "I can't believe we have to go back to school tomorrow."

"Better than being trapped in a mirror," Raphael said as he sat on a stool behind the counter.

"Speaking of mirrors, I wonder how Milo is. Mr. McGuire spent all day on the phone talking to people about getting him out. No luck so far. But there are going to be a ton of questions from everyone in class about the show."

"If we stick to the plan, everything will be okay," Raphael said. "We tell them we were asked to be in the benefit. I'll talk about the hidden harness, and you'll talk about the mirrors that made it look like you were able to transport yourself across the stage. And if Fiona says anything, who'll believe her?"

"We'll have to tell her the truth and somehow get her to forgive us."

"Us?"

"Okay, me."

Raphael smiled. "Hey, I've got your back—that's what us sidekicks are for. Once *we* talk to her, I think she'll come around. I mean, who wouldn't want a *magician* for a best friend? You'd be a huge help to her in the upcoming election. But the really big question is, are you going to tell your grandmother what you did?"

I frowned and put the sloshing jar of starfish legs I was jiggling back on the shelf. "You mean, about my parents?"

"Yeah, are you going to tell her you zapped their memories?"

"I think finding out I'm a magician was traumatic enough, don't you?"

"What if Hasenpfeffer tells her? He's not exactly good at keeping his mouth shut."

"I've threatened him with a smaller cage. He's not going to talk."

Hasenpfeffer looked up from the pile of Timothy hay he was eating. "She also said she'd take away my snuggy-blanket. The girl clearly has issues." He hopped over to Raphael. *"I may be in danger,"* he whispered not so softly.

Raphael eyed me suspiciously. "Threatening a poor defenseless rabbit? My, my, don't you sound like a certain evil magician. You and Milo didn't switch brains, did you?"

"Ha, ha. Look, I know I've made a few mistakes, more than you know, but I think I have a better handle on things now. Despite almost landing in a magic mirror for the rest of my life, hanging around with Milo was actually a good thing. I know I need to use my power more carefully. I can't just—you know—change people for my convenience. Which will make school more interesting. Fiona and I are going to have to start using our heads a lot more." I bit my lip. "And I have a confession to make."

"You used your magic to make me stay so you wouldn't be alone with Milo the day he gave you the book."

"You knew?"

"Of course I knew; I am a certified genius, after all. One second I was totally mad and ready to race you to Mr. McGuire's, and then the next moment I'm all, like, 'Yeah, I'll stay.' I knew you were messing with my mind. Well, I *suspected* you were. After Hasenpfeffer spilled the beans about your parents, I was sure. "

"I'm really sorry, and I promise I'll never ever do that again." I picked up a jar of spiders and gave it a couple of shakes. "Oops!" I said as their legs broke off and fell to the bottom.

"Are you going to tell Mr. McGuire you shook his spiders to pieces?"

I rolled my eyes. "I will confess to destroying a jar of freeze-dried spiders."

Mr. McGuire walked into the shop, carrying the mail. "Maggie, be careful, those are very delicate."

"Too late," Raphael said.

Mr. McGuire sighed. "Let's see what this is." He held out a package at arm's length and squinted at the label. "It's from Reginald." He used a small knife to open up the package, and pulled out a picture book. *"Barty Bananas Goes to the Moon."* He flipped through the first pages. "It's autographed to you, Maggie, and there's a note."

I jumped off the ladder, and Mr. McGuire handed me a letter. "I scanned the letter and smiled. "Reginald's *sister* is the author of the Barty Bananas books. That explains why he was such a big fan."

The repair shop door opened suddenly, and I gaped as Mrs. Davenport and Darcy stalked in wearing matching pink tops and lime green skirts. Mrs. Davenport glared at all of us and then started to clap her hands slowly.

"Bravo, all of you. That was quite the impressive show you put on yesterday."

Darcy smiled with evil glee.

"I'm sure I don't know what you mean," Mr. McGuire said.

Hasenpfeffer stood up on his haunches and then raced into the back room.

"We were at the benefit I set up to watch my beloved cousin Milo's performance."

"Cousin?" I said.

"To say we were shocked to see you onstage and then trapping dear Milo in a shard of glass is putting it mildly."

My stomach flip-flopped. If Darcy was Milo's cousin, Darcy was a magician too.

Mr. McGuire snapped his suspenders. "Well, I can assure you that anything that transpired was all of Milo's doing. He tried to send Maggie into the mirror, despite knowing the duplicate he had created was powerless."

Mrs. Davenport fluffed her hair. "Well, we'll see about that. If there was any misconduct, Viola Klemp will have this"—she raised her nose in the air and looked around—"establishment closed in a heartbeat."

"I've filed a full report," Mr. McGuire said.

"*As have I*," Mrs. Davenport hissed.

Mr. McGuire snapped his suspenders again. "I'm *confident* there won't be any charges filed."

"Perhaps," she drawled. "But there is the matter of Maggie's conduct at school. Darcy thinks she's been ignoring the magical betterment guidelines and using her powers to assist herself and her friend."

Mr. McGuire turned to me. "I'm sure you're mistaken."

"I'm sure I'm not!" snapped Darcy.

"I-I didn't know there were rules," I stammered. "No one told me."

Mr. McGuire took his glasses off his nose and rubbed his eyes. "She didn't know, Ms—"

"*Mrs. Davenport.*"

Mr. McGuire paled. "Mrs. Davenport, so *nice* to put a face to the name, but Maggie clearly falls under section seven of the magical conduct code. Her parents are nonmagical, as is her grandmother, so they weren't aware of all the bylaws. I will personally take charge of her education and notify Viola myself about any transgressions, so we can put this silly misunderstanding behind us."

Mrs. Davenport gave us a cold smile. "I'll leave that up to the board to decide how *silly* this all is. Come, Darcy, we have a Labor Day party to host."

She headed toward the door, and Darcy turned to

Raphael and me. "You'd better be careful, Bug Girl, because I will be watching your every move."

I leaned in close to her. "And I'll be watching you, too," I said. "I have a feeling Nahla's science fair project had some help self-destructing. And that comet you found—it reeks of magic."

Darcy's mouth dropped as a flush came to her pale cheeks.

"Come along, Darcy," Mrs. Davenport said from the door.

"See you Tuesday," I called out with a wave.

Mr. McGuire let out a long breath as they walked up the stairs to the street. "Cousin Milo, just our luck. Mrs. Davenport is very influential in the magical community here."

My heart raced. "Are we in trouble?"

"I think everything will be all right, but you may have to talk to Viola. Given the situation, I can't imagine they'd petition to strip your powers."

"Strip my powers?"

"No need worrying, I'm sure everything will turn out fine."

"I'd worry!" Hasenpfeffer whispered as he hopped out of the back room. "I knew I recognized the name Davenport—I've seen those two before, and they're *bad* news."

"Why?" Raphael asked.

Hasenpfeffer shook his head and chattered his teeth. "That girl, I've, I've heard her speak of the most *horrible* things."

Raphael and I exchanged looks. "What kind of things?" we said together.

Hasenpfeffer shuddered. "I *accidentally* bit her one time when she was visiting Milo. She threatened to skin me and use my paws for lucky rabbit's feet!" He ran in circles and wailed. "Can you imagine anything more horrible?"

"You bit her?"

He held up one paw a bit. "Just a tiny nip, it only bled for a few minutes—nothing a Band-Aid and some applied pressure couldn't take care of. But don't bother casting any friendship spells or such on her. She wears a locket that Milo gave her. It protects her from being magically influenced."

I groaned. "That's why she was the only person who wasn't happy when I suggested everyone should consider Fiona as the best candidate for president."

Mr. McGuire clucked his tongue. "Just how many spells did you cast at school?"

"I kind of lost count."

"Maybe if we figured out a way to free Milo, the

Davenports would lighten up a little," Raphael suggested.

"Oh, doubtful," Hasenpfeffer said. "It's all the same with those non-showbiz magicians. They always have something to prove—and hide. Keeping all that magic bottled up just causes trouble with a capital T! Uh, no offense to you, McGuire; you're the exception to that rule, I'm sure."

Mr. McGuire rolled his eyes. "And freeing Milo might not be good for our health, but I'm still digging up more information on the mirror to see if we can help him. Viola has asked some people to look into it as well."

Otto jumped off a shelf and stretched his long legs on the counter.

"What about Otto?" I asked.

"I'm in no rush to repair him. Dagmar was a bit shaken from the whole duplicate business and decided to take some time off and travel. Otto will stay with us until she gets back."

I leaned against the counter and rubbed my eyes. "I can't believe *Darcy Davenport* is a magician too."

"And you're a magician who knows she can't be throwing wishes and spells around whenever she wants," Mr. McGuire said.

I looked away. "I know," I said.

But with the class election coming up, reconnecting with Fiona, and keeping up with school, the big question was—how could I stop myself?

Get a sneak peek of
the second book in the series,
THE SHAPE-SHIFTERS CURSE

A s soon as Gram left the apartment Sunday morning to work at the food pantry, I raced to my room and slipped on my shoes. After everything that had happened in the last week, Gram had decided the magic repair shop was too dangerous and I was forbidden to go there *ever again*. But I knew I couldn't stay away. I *had* to get Mr. McGuire to convince Gram to let me work there.

That's not to say I didn't understand why Gram didn't want me to go down to the shop anymore. I'd been in Connecticut for less than a week and had already been attacked by a lion and kidnapped by a crazed magician, and just last night I was seconds away from spending the rest of my life in a magic mirror.

Getting her to change her mind was going to be harder than teaching an elephant to ride a unicycle on a tightrope.

I grabbed my keys off my night table and bumped Hasenpfeffer's cage. Grimacing, I crossed my fingers and hoped I hadn't woken him up.

"For pity's sake," he snapped. He poked his furry, white head out from under his blanket, blinking his pink eyes in the light. "Can't a rabbit take a nap in peace?"

"Sorry."

"You're always *sorry*, Maggie," he continued. "How about you just watch where those enormous feet of yours are going."

"They're only a size four!"

Hasenpfeffer sat up on his haunches. "Yet they somehow *always* manage to hit my cage."

I rolled my eyes. There'd been more than one occasion I'd regretted casting the spell that gave him speech—even if it had been by accident—and this was one of them. "*Fine*, I'll move your cage away from my bed where I won't bang into it."

I looked around the tiny bedroom I'd be staying in for the next year while my parents were hunting cockroaches in the Amazon. There weren't a lot of options. "How about over there, by the window?"

Hasenpfeffer peered at the window overlooking the street below. "What and get heatstroke when the afternoon sun comes in? No, thank you."

I pointed to the other side of the room by my closet.

He shook his head. "Too drafty."

"By the computer?"

"What, and listen to that infernal humming all the time? Tsk. There really isn't a good spot in this shoebox of a room." He chattered his teeth as he sniffed around, peering into every corner. "I'm not used to being in such confined quarters all the time. I miss the grand hotel rooms I stayed in when Milo and I traveled—I miss performing and hearing the cheers as I got pulled out of the hat. Look what's become of me. Stuck here with nothing to do all day but stare at an overabundance of unicorn posters."

He sniffed, and I wondered if it was possible for a rabbit to cry.

"I never imagined I'd retire this early," he continued, "but I thought if I ever did, I'd be living it up in a spacious hutch in Japan. Milo and I were *very* popular in Japan. I even got fan mail." He let out a long, mournful sigh.

I decided not to remind him he was stuck with me

because his former owner, Milo the Magnificent, had *abandoned* him in the magic repair shop. The fact that Milo had tried to kill me, apparently had no effect on Hasenpfeffer's longing for his old life.

"Well, I'm going for a walk," I said, trying to sound light and breezy. "Tell Gram if she gets home before I do, okay?"

"Oh please. You're going to the shop. And don't pretend otherwise." He shook his head. "You're a *terrible* actress."

"I'm not going to the shop!" I lied. "I'm just going for a walk. You know—fresh air, sunshine."

"I demand parsley or I tell the old woman you're with McGuire."

"That's blackmail," I said, putting my hands on my hips.

He put a paw on his nearly empty food dish. "Call it what you want, but it would be *very* easy to forget this conversation ever happened if I had a belly full of parsley."

I squeezed my eyes tight. "Fine. You win."

"Make it the flat-leaf Italian parsley. It's my favorite and easier on my digestive system."

I shook my head as I took out my grandfather's old wooden wand—curved and bent like a tree branch—from my desk drawer. After working out a simple rhyme in my head, I pointed the wand at Hasenpfeffer's cage. "Garden's growing rather sparsely, let's just get a crop of parsley." A shower of green sparks shot out from the tip, and then Hasenpfeffer's bowl was filled to the top with parsley.

He hopped over and sniffed. "Ah. Perfect." He grabbed a mouthful and started chewing noisily. "Tell McGuire I said hello," he mumbled.